I0573448

WATCH OVER ME

A SMALL TOWN ROMANTIC SUSPENSE

KAIT NOLAN

Watch Over Me

Copyright © 2018 by Kait Nolan

All rights reserved.

No part of this book may be reproduced in any form or by any electronic or mechanical means, including information storage and retrieval systems, without written permission from the author, except for the use of brief quotations in a book review.

When you feel crazy, it's the ones who love you anyway who matter most

A LETTER TO READERS

Dear Reader,

This book is set in the Deep South. As such, it contains a great deal of colorful, colloquial, and occasionally grammatically incorrect language. This is a deliberate choice on my part as an author to most accurately represent the region where I have lived my entire life. This book also contains swearing and pre-marital sex between the lead couple, as those things are part of the realistic lives of characters of this generation, and of many of my readers.

If any of these things are not your cup of

tea, please consider that you may not be the right audience for this book. There are scores of other books out there that are written with you in mind. In fact, I've got a list of some of my favorite authors who write on the sweeter side on my website at https://kaitnolan.com/on-the-sweeter-side/

If you choose to stick with me, I hope you enjoy!

Happy reading!

Kait

CHAPTER 1

Rowan Beale glanced at the clock on the wall and fought to keep her expression neutral, her posture relaxed. She'd had enough of these sessions to know that any sign of impatience or resistance would prompt Dr. Powers to extend their time together, trying to unearth the root of the discomfort. Rowan would rather have bamboo shoved under her fingernails than continue to have this woman explore her psyche. But the department had its rules, and as the in-house shrink, Tisha Powers had all the control. Without her go ahead, Rowan wasn't getting off the desk she'd been riding for the past two months. So, she'd play nice.

"How are you feeling today, Rowan?"

"Fine." A lie, but the truth would keep her on the desk.

One blonde brow arched, telling Rowan that Dr. Powers didn't buy it. "What did you do this weekend?"

For once, she had something to report. "I went to a birthday party."

"Going out with friends is an excellent step." Dr. Powers' voice had the kind of bright tone one used to praise a dog for good behavior.

Rowan had to fight the urge to tense her shoulders in irritation. "It was for Anna Sofia. She turned three." And David hadn't been there to see it. Just like he wouldn't be there for any other of his daughter's birthdays ever again. Rowan's throat went thick, but she swallowed against it. "Stacy had me over to help wrangle the pack of tiny humans."

That David's wife could even look at

Rowan, let alone still speak to her, was a constant amazement. Stacy didn't blame her for David's death. Maybe someday Rowan would manage to believe that. For now, she was still caught up in the fresh hell of *what if*, playing that horrible night over and over, wondering what she could've done differently, how she could've stopped it.

Dr. Powers smiled. "And how did that go?"

"I'd rather face off with a group of gangbangers than a herd of toddlers. They're relentless and impossible to negotiate with. I will have the music from *Frozen* stuck in my head for the next month. Maybe longer."

"Can't let it go?"

Really? Dr. Powers was gonna make a joke? They didn't have that kind of relationship. And damn it, now that song was running through her head again. She probably shouldn't flip off her therapist. "Thanks for that earworm," she said flatly.

"Sorry." Dr. Powers' pale pink lips twitched

before returning to her usual concerned expression. "How are you sleeping?"

"A little better." That, at least, was true. She hadn't woken screaming for the past week. "Things have been quiet."

The moment those pale blue eyes sharpened, Rowan knew she shouldn't have said that. "You've had no further...incidents?"

"I've had no further harassment," Rowan corrected. She could only assume that was because she'd kept her mouth shut and her head down. She was still persona non grata in the department. That's what happened when you made accusations against one of your own. Accusations that remained unsubstantiated.

"You still believe someone is targeting you."

Rowan wrestled with her need for the truth versus her desire to be done with this bullshit and sent back out on duty. Apparently, her silence was answer enough.

Dr. Powers folded her hands. "You've made progress these past couple of months, Rowan. But I still believe you have work to do. I'm not sure you can really do that work while en-sconced within a department where you feel persecuted and not trusted."

The first hints of panic scrabbled up Rowan's throat. "What are you saying?"

"I'm recommending you for a period of mandatory leave."

Rowan exploded out of the chair. "That's bullshit!"

Dr. Powers didn't react to her outburst. "You've been through so much since Officer Reyes's death. And with the other incidents, I simply don't feel you are presently fit for duty."

"You can't do this. You can't take this away from me." Rowan didn't know who she was when she wasn't a cop.

"This isn't a punishment."

The hell it wasn't. "I passed all my certs. Fit-ness. Firearms."

"But you're not passing the psychological evaluation. You're a powder keg, Rowan. You're still struggling to process what happened to your partner, still in denial about it. You've been given a perfectly reasonable explanation for the things you heard, yet you refuse to believe it. You cling to your version of events because you need someone to blame for Officer Reyes's death."

She clung to her version because it was the truth.

"You need to take some time."

"I need to get back to work." *I need to feel normal.* "I'm going to talk to the captain about it."

"Feel free. But he won't go against my recommendation."

She was right and they both knew it. But Rowan couldn't just sit by and take this without a fight. Before she could start for the door, her phone rang.

Grateful for any kind of interruption, she yanked it out.

"Oh, now really. We've talked about having your phone silenced in session," Dr. Powers chided.

Seeing her mother's name flash on the

screen, Rowan ignored the therapist and answered. "Hey, Mom."

"Rowan." The single word, uttered in a voice strangled by tears had her going stock still.

"Mom? What's wrong?"

Her mother took a shuddering breath. "It's your Uncle Robert, honey. He's had another heart attack."

Her gut took a swan dive. "What? No. He was better. He's been doing what he was supposed to after the last one."

"That's what we thought. But he's had another. A bad one, this time. They're taking him into surgery now. Your grandfather and I are on our way to Lawley."

"Lawley. Not Wishful?"

"They needed a specialist."

Rowan closed her eyes and began to pray. If anything happened to Robert... Sucking in a breath, she opened her eyes and looked at Dr. Powers. "I'm on my way. I've got some leave time coming."

"Good. That's good. Nash is flying to get you. He's on his way to the airfield now."

The ex-Navy pilot was her great uncle's neighbor and had been one of his reserve officers before he'd retired as Chief of Police in Wishful. They'd met when Rowan had come after the first heart attack a couple months ago. If he was flying all the way to Houston to pick her up, it must be bad.

"Does he have my number?"

"Yes. He'll text you when his flight plan is in place."

"Okay." She took a breath and reached for calm. "Okay, I'm headed home to pack. I'll see you soon."

Without another word to Dr. Powers, Rowan strode out of her office. She had a more important mission right now.

NASH BREWER FOUGHT against a wicked headwind to maintain control of his little

Cessna 210 Centurion, Diana. All that extra moisture being sucked in from the Gulf of Mexico gave the storm teeth and a helluva bad temper. But it wasn't the first bad weather he'd flown in, and it certainly wouldn't be the last. He had a mission, and he'd be damned if he'd fail. Robert's family was counting on him.

By the time the landing strip came into view, beads of cold sweat had traced their way down his spine, dampening his shirt beneath the battered leather jacket. After a brief conversation with the tower, he made his approach, dropping the landing gear, adjusting the flaps as he dropped Diana toward the ground. She bucked a bit but settled on the runway with a single skip. Slowing her pace, he taxied to where he'd been ordered and parked.

"Welcome to Houston." Nash patted the instrument panel. "Good girl. I'm gonna let you suck down some more juice, pick up our passenger, and we're gonna head straight back home."

The weather on the ground was no more

hospitable than the sky. Rain lashed the tarmac in gusts that were almost horizontal. Sane people weren't flying in this shit. But there was a reason he'd been dubbed Loco during his years in the Navy. He preferred to think of himself as having balls of steel.

He turned his phone back on and sent a quick text to Rowan. **Just touched down. You here yet?**

Her answer came back immediately. **In the terminal.**

Nash: **Gotta refuel. Liftoff in twenty.**

He took care of gassing Diana up and navigated her toward the main terminal. With the weather being what it was, he didn't have to fight for space. He'd go in to get Rowan, help with her luggage. The wind tried to tear the cockpit door out of his hand. Nash fought it back in place and wished he'd packed rain gear. He was soaked in seconds. Resigned, he trudged toward the small, glass-front building.

One of the doors swung open and a woman stepped into the storm, a large duffel thrown over her shoulder. Even at this distance, he recognized that fall of dark brown hair. As he should. He'd spent plenty of time itching to run his hands through it during her last visit. He hurried forward to meet her.

"You'd think one of us would've had the sense to pack an umbrella." He had to shout to be heard over the roar of the wind.

"Wasn't a priority." Her lush mouth was set in a grim line.

Nash saw in an instant that she'd lost weight since September, and the dark circles under her sky-blue eyes were deeper than she'd have simply from the shock and worry over her uncle. What had happened to her in the last few months? Had she been ill?

"Has there been any news since I took off?"

"He's in surgery now. They said it could take up to six hours."

"Then we may be back before he's out."

"Are we ready to go?" she asked.

"Soon as we get on board. Here, let me take your bag."

"I've got it." Rowan brushed past him, hoofing it toward the plane.

Well, okay then. Nash followed. She did have to give it over so he could stow it for the flight. He helped her inside. "You want to ride up front with me?" Not that the little four-seater offered a lot of options.

"Front's fine."

They settled in. Nash cleared takeoff with the tower, turning all his attention on his instrument panel and the stretch of runway in front of him.

"Hold on to your butt. This may be a bit of a bumpy takeoff."

Rowan said nothing, but he caught the whitening of her knuckles on the armrest of her seat as they left the ground and wobbled. "C'mon, baby. Settle down."

"Excuse me?"

"Not you, the plane."

"Is it safe to fly in this storm?"

Nash gave her props for the conversational

tone. "I've flown in worse. Don't worry. I'll get you back to Lawley all in one piece."

Rowan lapsed into silence again. Half an hour into the flight, he managed to climb above the worst of the storm to some calmer air. Beside him, Rowan exhaled. "That's better."

"This storm is a slow-moving bastard. In another twenty minutes or so, we'll be out of it entirely."

"It always rains the day a good man dies."

Startled, he glanced over at her. "What?"

"Somebody I knew said that once. Seems like he's usually right." Her blue eyes were haunted as she said it, and Nash wondered who she'd lost. Was grief what had winnowed her down since he'd seen her last?

"Robert's not gonna die." He didn't know that, not for sure. But the alternative wasn't something Nash could contemplate right this second.

"He might."

"They've got one of the best cardiac surgeons

in the state working on him. It was a bad attack, but bypass surgery is commonly done. There's every reason to believe he's going to pull through."

"I just don't understand what happened. He was in good shape when I left him in September. He was following doctor's orders, getting rest, easing back into exercise." Rowan fixed her gaze on him. "You've been there with him. Has he been eating right? Overdoing it?"

"Well, I haven't been policing his food, but I haven't seen him shoveling in chili cheese fries and double cheeseburgers. As to whether he's overdoing it...I don't know. He's been feeling good. Restless, but that's to be expected. He didn't want to retire."

"No, he didn't. A cop who's not a cop doesn't know how to behave."

There was something in her tone that had him glancing over, but Rowan wasn't looking at him.

"What the hell is a man like him supposed to do with retirement?" she demanded. "He's not even sixty."

"I don't know. Heal up from this, for starters." But Nash knew as well as she did that Robert Curry was not a man who tended toward idleness. He'd been bored during his recovery. Nash had tried to look out for him, but there was every possibility he'd done something he shouldn't have when nobody was watching.

Nash squelched the trickle of guilt. "Look, you're worried. So am I. But Robert is a tough old bastard. He's not going down without a fight."

Please, dear God, don't let him make a liar out of me.

CHAPTER 2

*H*e's out of surgery.

The text hit Rowan's phone as soon as she turned it back on in Lawley. Some of the tension that had dogged her since her mother called leeched out of her shoulders. "Thank God. He's out."

Nash shot her a smile. "See there. I told you he'd be fine."

Surviving bypass surgery was probably a long way from fine, but she appreciated his optimism. He'd kept her calm on the harrowing flight from Houston. "I appreciate you coming to get me."

"No problem. Let me just get Diana squared away in the hangar, and we'll get on to the hospital."

"Diana?"

"The plane. That's her name. After Wonder Woman."

Rowan looked over at him. "You named your plane after a superhero?"

His grin was a quick flash of white against the dark, close-cropped beard. "Damn straight."

"Why her instead of, like, Superman or something?"

"First, planes are female. As are cars, boats, and most other forms of machinery."

"Everyone knows that."

"Yeah, well, even if they weren't, I'd still have chosen Diana because she kicks all their asses *and* is a symbol for optimism. When you're in the middle of dicey conditions, you want that optimism as a pilot."

"Fair enough." Rowan wondered if he'd been this naturally optimistic in the Navy.

While Nash did whatever post-flight check stuff was necessary to his plane, Rowan took the time to make herself a little more presentable. Her clothes had dried stiff and uncomfortable. As the stuff in her duffel was also damp, there wasn't much she could do about that, but she tamed her hair into a braid and slapped on a little makeup to cover up the bruising under her eyes. Her mom and grandfather hadn't seen her since Reyes's death. At least not since she'd gotten out of the hospital herself. She didn't want them worrying.

Half an hour later, she strode through the utilitarian hallways of Wachoxee County Hospital, Nash by her side. Her mother had texted that they were on the third floor, Room 318. Eager to see for herself that Robert was okay and itching to work off some of the nervous energy, she bypassed the elevator in favor of the fire stairs. Nash followed without comment.

When they reached the third-floor landing, he grabbed her hand. "Hold up a sec."

Startled by the touch, she looked back at him. "What?"

"Take a minute to breathe. You don't want to go in there looking like the devil's on your heels."

"I need to see for myself that he's okay." Because while they were en route from the airport, she'd been imagining him taking a turn for the worse.

"I know. But just go with it. Deep breaths."

Impatient, and realizing he wasn't going to let her out of this stairwell until she listened to him, Rowan matched her breath to his, sucking in deep lungfuls of air on a count of four and exhaling on a count of eight as she focused on his warm brown eyes. In and out. In and out. Oddly, she felt some of the rough edges smooth a bit.

"There. That's better." His lips curved.

"Thanks." Rowan realized he hadn't let go of her hand about the same time he did. They both looked down at their tangle of fingers for a moment. Then he released her and tugged open the door.

Their wet shoes squeaked on the industrial tile floor, sounding too loud in the otherwise muted environment of the hospital. Turning the corner, she saw her mom and grandfather standing with a white-coated doctor and broke into a run.

"Is he all right?"

Granddad reached out an arm and pulled her into his side. "My granddaughter, Rowan. This is Dr. Evers."

The doctor, a fifty-something man with a salt-and-pepper beard and one of those medical do-rags over his hair, offered a kind smile. "Mr. Curry came through surgery just fine. I was just letting your family know what he's going to need these next few weeks."

"Is he awake?"

"Groggy and a little muzzy-headed, but that's to be expected. You can see him in a little bit. As I was saying. He'll definitely need someone staying with him at home for the next couple of weeks. No driving for four to six weeks. The motion of turning the wheel will pull at his incision. He's encouraged to move around, not too fast, but building up to more activity as he feels up to it. He can still do light chores, but no lifting anything heavier than five to seven pounds."

"How long until he's back to normal?" Mom asked.

"Barring complications, he'll be back to more independence in six weeks. It'll be two to three months before he's really back to normal."

Granddad frowned. "Do you have recommendations for a home health service? Neither of us is able to take off work that long."

Rowan jumped in. "I'll do it." When her mom and grandfather stared at her, she just shrugged. "I have the time, and there's nothing more important to me than his recovery."

They exchanged a worried look, and she knew she hadn't done as good as job as she'd hoped with the makeup. Thank God they only knew Reyes had been killed and not the rest of it. Forcing a lightness she didn't feel, Rowan smiled. "Besides, I'm the only one of us as tough as he is."

"I can certainly help."

Nash. None of them had noticed when he'd joined them.

Rowan's mother immediately wrapped him in a hug. "Thank you so much for going to get Rowan."

"Of course. No sense having a pilot in your pocket if you don't take advantage when you need it."

His good-humored smile flashed, and Rowan was beyond grateful that he'd offered his services to get her here. She turned her attention back to the doctor. "Can we see him?"

"For just a little while. He'll need to rest. I'll pull together some materials on everything you need to know about his post-op care, the things you need to do to prepare for him to come home in a few days."

"How long will he need to stay here?" Granddad asked.

"Three to eight days, depending."

Which meant she'd be here for probably three weeks at the very least. Dr. Powers would approve. And maybe she was right, at least a little. Maybe the time away from Houston, away from the department and the looks of distrust, the muttered remarks, and the veiled threats would be good for her. Maybe she'd finally have a chance to properly grieve for her partner and figure out what to do next. And when nothing happened here, Dr. Powers would be forced to acknowledge that the problem was inside the department, not Rowan's head.

Rowan left her parents talking to the doctor and slipped into the room. Her great uncle was hooked up to all kinds of monitors. The sight of him in that hospital bed, his pallor gray, oxygen tubes draping a face that seemed to have aged ten years since she saw him last, was a sucker punch to the gut. He'd always been such a vital, bigger than life figure. Now, for the first time in her life, he looked old. It scared the shit out of her.

"Roo?"

At the sound of his childhood nickname for her, Rowan moved toward the bed to take his hand, plastering a cheerful smile on her face. "Hey there, Unk."

He studied her through heavy eyes. "You look like shit."

That surprised a laugh out of her. "Back atcha. You scared everybody."

"Lotta fuss over nothing."

"It was a bit more than nothing. But you're gonna be fine, now. I'm gonna see to it."

"Are you now?"

"Yep. You're looking at your new roommate, old man."

"Roommate or warden?"

"Maybe a little of both." Because she didn't know where else she could touch him without hurting anything, she brought their joined hands to her cheek. "Don't be a grumpy cuss. Let me take care of you for once."

He heaved a put-upon sigh. "Fine, but I get control of the remote."

That was her Uncle Robert. This time the smile was genuine. "I can work with that."

NASH WHEELED his truck into his driveway. After this week's hop-and-skip to Atlanta, his bank account would be fat enough to stay put for a few days. He wanted a change of clothes, a beer, and to check in on his new neighbor. He'd hated leaving town right after getting her settled. Not that Rowan was exactly asking for his help. But he'd worried about her while he was away. Other than a daily text update on Robert's progress, she'd been incommunicado since he dropped her off from the hospital. Was she home or was she still in Lawley for her daily pilgrimage?

As if conjured by his thoughts, his phone began to ring, and her name flashed across the screen. Hitting answer, Nash paused on his

own front porch to look out across the long expanse of acreage toward Robert's place. "I was
just about to call you."

There was a beat of hesitation. "Oh yeah?"

"I wanted to see what the update was on
Robert." And yeah, okay, he wanted to see how
she was doing, too. She'd been pretty damned
ragged when he'd dropped her off from the
hospital the other day.

"He's improving nicely. Doc says, barring
any complications, he can come home tomorrow. I'm working on getting the house ready."

"Need a hand?"

After the I-can-do-it-myself attitude she'd
shown at the airport, he was surprised when
she said, "That's actually why I was calling. I
saw your truck drive by. You busy this
evening?"

Had she been watching for him to get back?
Nah. That was probably wishful thinking on his
part. "Not particularly. Whatcha need?"

"A strong back and an appetite."

"Funny, I've got both of those."

"Well, if you want to head on over this way in a bit, I'll put you to work, then feed you for your trouble. The house is full of a bunch of junk Robert can't eat, and I'd hate for it to go to waste. I could use some help devouring it before he gets home."

The prospect of spending the evening with her was way more appealing than it should be. She was Robert's niece. Or...great niece? Nash wasn't entirely clear on that. Either way, she was only here temporarily. A smart man would steer clear of any entanglements.

Nobody had ever accused Nash of being smart.

"Bribery by food is always acceptable. I'll be over in ten."

He changed clothes and made it in five.

Rowan answered the door in ancient jeans and a long-sleeved, V-neck t-shirt that did nothing to hide the fact that she was a woman. The ultra-soft cotton hugged the curves of her breasts in a way that had his eyes wanting to do the same. Ruthlessly, he forced his gaze up to scan her face. The dark circles were nearly gone, and her blue eyes were bright and alert—and amused as she caught him noticing her.

"You look better." The moment the words were out of his mouth, Nash wished them back. "Sorry, I just mean you looked pretty strung out and worried when I picked you up the other day. Now you don't."

Her own gaze raked him from head to toe as she backed up and motioned him inside. "It's a fair observation. I've de-stressed over the past few days, now that I know Robert is going to be okay. I've been sleeping like a rock. It's peaceful out here."

"I imagine anything away from Houston seems peaceful."

Her shoulders went rigid. "What's that supposed to mean?"

Nash frowned wondering what he'd said wrong. "Nothing. You live in a city that has a bigger population than the entire state of Mississippi. I can't fathom finding much peace with that many people crammed into such a small space."

"Oh. Yeah." Rowan exhaled and seemed to force herself to relax. "Ignore me. I'm still a little rattled."

On edge is what she was, and it had nothing to do with Robert. As a born fixer, Nash had an insatiable need to poke and pry. He and Rowan didn't have that kind of relationship—or any relationship, really—so he let the odd behavior go. But it didn't stop the itch of curiosity.

"So, I'm guessing we're starting with the strong back stuff?"

"Yeah, in the bedroom."

Nash blinked, grateful she'd already headed down the hall so she didn't see the instant punch of lust. *Down boy.*

But the caution did nothing to stop his eyes from fixing on the shape of her ass as she walked. Officer Beale was in prime physical shape. If he appreciated that, he was only human.

"I want to move one of the chairs from the

living room in here, so he has somewhere he can sit to put on socks and shoes or whatever. Not that he'll be doing that on his own for a bit, but it's part and parcel of the whole."

Nash stepped into a bedroom. It looked like Robert—confirmed bachelor. He'd moved into this house after his divorce and never had a woman touch it. The bed was made with a plain, hunter green spread. The windows had some out-of-the-package plaid curtains that were apparently made to match the comforter. They still had creases from where they'd been folded. Nash had a similar set in his place, though his mom had ironed them on some previous visit. The Mission-style furniture was utilitarian and functional—no muss, no fuss. Stacks and stacks of clothes covered the queen-size bed.

"What on earth are you doing?"

"Reorganizing his closet. He's got a lot of his everyday stuff on high-up shelves he won't be able to stretch to reach, and he won't be able to wear shirts without buttons for a while, so I'm moving stuff and sorting things in order of most likely to be used."

"Sensible."

"I'll get that finished later. For now, I need to shift the dresser down a few feet to make room for the chair in that corner, but I didn't want to scratch the hardwood floors."

"My back is yours, milady."

They took care of the dresser, then hauled in the chair. She added a throw and a pillow she'd unearthed from who knew where and declared it done.

"That's a nice homey touch. But what about the hole in the living room now? The seating is kinda sparse."

Rowan shot him a grin that gave him a hint of the woman she was when she wasn't beaten down by stress and worry. "I bought him the Cadillac of recliners. It's out in the truck."

"You bought Robert a recliner?"

"Yep. This may be the most comfortable chair I've ever sat in."

"You know he calls those old man chairs, right? He's refused to get one."

"Please. The man's going to be in love with it in the end."

"And if he's not?"

"Then once he's healed up, I'll take it home myself."

She led him out to Robert's truck where The Chair waited to be hauled in. It was definitely a capital letter piece of furniture.

"Are those cupholders?"

Her grin flashed again. "Yes. Yes, they are."

"Hang on, I need a minute." Nash laid a hand over his heart and bowed his head, both in homage to The Chair and to the woman who'd actually bought it.

Rowan laughed, looped her arm through his and gave it a squeeze. "You can genuflect after we get it inside. C'mon."

It took some serious muscle. The Chair was a massive bastard and getting it through the door wasn't an easy task. But at last, they got it in place, in prime view of the TV and the big picture window that overlooked the woods stretching behind the house.

Rowan gestured toward The Chair. "Go ahead. Take it for a test drive."

Nash flopped down, appreciating the way the cushy leather cupped his body. He ran his hands over the arms. "This is a glorious piece of furniture."

"The doctor warned me that the bed might not be comfortable for him and that patients often find recliners easier to sleep in, so I figured it was worth getting him a good one."

"It's huge. Like, there's room for two people in here." On impulse, he grabbed her around the waist and sprang the footrest.

Rowan tumbled onto him with a yelp, her legs tangling with his, her face ending up millimeters from his. To test his luck, Nash settled a hand against her lower back, letting one thumb stroke against the skin exposed where her t-shirt rode up.

"See, plenty of room," he murmured.

She planted a hand against his chest but

didn't move away. "Are you flirting with me, Nash?"

"If you have to ask, I'm doing a terrible job of it."

The mouth that hovered so tantalizingly close to his quirked a little. "I'm flattered."

"But?"

"There are probably a hundred reasons why pursuing that would be a bad idea."

"Probably," he agreed. When she still didn't push him away, he risked sliding his palm more fully under her shirt to span the warm expanse of her back. "Do you actually care about any of them?"

"Having a hard time thinking about why I should just now." It was her slightly breathless tone that did him in.

"Me too." Nash slid his free hand into her hair and brought her mouth to his.

CHAPTER 3

The very last thing Rowan had expected to be doing tonight was making out with Nash Brewer in the monster recliner. It was ridiculous. Juvenile, even. She didn't let men get close—a consequence of being a woman in a male-dominated profession, even before everything went to shit. But the moment Nash settled his mouth over hers, all she wanted was to get closer. It was impossible to *think* like this, with his lips exploring hers. It had been so long since she'd been able to turn off her brain and escape.

On a sigh, she opened for him, angling her head to take the kiss deeper, committing to oblivion for just a little while. She let go of everything else but the feel and flavor of him, unfamiliar and exciting. He tasted of coffee and something darker that didn't quite match the easygoing flyboy persona he usually wore. The combination lit a spark in her blood.

She tunneled her hand under his shirt, over the hard ridges of his abs, feeling them contract beneath her touch. It made her smile against his mouth. A groan rumbled through him, wringing an answering moan from her. His hands slid down her back and over her butt, hooking under her thighs and dragging her until she straddled his hips. As the bulge in his jeans pressed against her center, the whole thing stopped feeling juvenile.

Rowan hissed in a breath as he rocked against her. God, *God* that felt amazing, even through two layers of jeans. She couldn't stop the hum of pleasure in her throat, couldn't keep from shifting against him, searching for a rhythm that would turn that spark to a full-on sizzle. His arms tightened around her, pulling her closer. *Oh yes, there.*

She couldn't remember the last time she'd been this turned on. Couldn't remember the last time anyone had touched her. There wasn't room for thought, wasn't room for anything but the feeling of giddy heat.

Nash's work-roughened hands slid beneath her shirt, playing over her back. What would those hands feel like on the rest of her? Obviously, he wanted to find out for himself, as he slid the shirt up to her shoulders, breaking the kiss so he could tug it over her head.

And just like that, her brain clicked back on.

Rowan froze, her shirt up around her ears. Beneath her, Nash went still, his hands fisted in the soft cotton.

"What the hell are we doing?" she whispered.

"By the look on your face right now, I'm gonna go with not getting naked." Gently, he smoothed the shirt back down.

Caught somewhere between relief and regret, Rowan couldn't seem to move.

When she said nothing, Nash turned to press a kiss to the forearm she'd braced by his head, keeping his eyes on hers. "Talk to me, Rowan."

Talk? What was she supposed to say? They'd been dry humping each other like a couple of teenagers. She'd been minutes away from doing a helluva lot more than that. The heat of her arousal now felt more like utter mortification.

"I—we—" How was she supposed to think while she still straddled his lap? "Let me up."

He reached for the lever to retract the footrest and suddenly they were upright again. His arm around her waist was the only thing that kept her from flying backward into the floor. She unfolded her legs, barely managing not to trip and fall in her haste to put some space between them.

"I need a minute."

Without waiting for an acknowledgment, she retreated to the kitchen. Because she still felt flushed and unsatisfied, she yanked open the fridge door and stuck her head inside, hoping the chill would help. It didn't. So, she grabbed one of the long-neck beers and ran the cold bottle along her heated skin, before twisting off the cap to take a long pull. As a rule, she didn't believe in alcohol for taking the edge off—she'd seen too many cops begin to use it as a crutch to handle the stress of the job. But tonight, she'd make an exception.

"Got another one of those?"

Rowan grabbed another bottle and handed it to him without quite meeting his eyes. He didn't press or invade her space, and she was grateful.

"I'm sorry. I wasn't trying to push. I just got carried away. I didn't mean to upset you."

"I'm not upset." At the lift of his brow she amended, "Or not exactly. I'm embarrassed."

"What's there to be embarrassed about? We're two consenting adults, who are apparently hot for each other."

The cheerfully factual way he stated it made

her laugh despite herself. "Yes, apparently we are."

If he wasn't going to be embarrassed, she could find it in herself to look him in the eye. "Nash, I don't do stuff like this."

"Make out like a horny teenager?" His grin said he definitely included himself in the horny teenager category.

He was incorrigible. Why was that so damned appealing?

"That. And I don't sleep with men I barely know."

Nodding, he took a pull on his beer. "Neither do I. And I just got very clear evidence that you're not a man, so I think we're safe."

She tried to give him a stern look. "I'm serious."

"So am I. Look, Rowan, I like you. I liked you when I met you back in September. You just weren't here long enough for me to do anything about it. For better or worse, you're here for a few weeks, and I'd like to get to know you better. Plus, I figure you could use a friend through all of this."

"Just a friend?"

He shrugged. "A friend. Somebody to get naked with and blow off steam. Whatever works for you. I'm not going to pressure you for more than you want to give. If you don't want me to touch you again, I won't. No harm, no foul. If you want to strip down and have hot monkey sex, I'm absolutely up for that, too."

Rowan stared at him. "Well, that's blunt."

"It's honest. My mama swears I have no tact, but I find that life usually runs smoother if you say what you mean."

"That's…"

His lips quirked in a wry smile. "Annoying?"

"Refreshing." She'd had little enough honesty these past few months. Tipping back her beer, she considered. Could she have a short, no-strings attached affair? She didn't know. She'd never done it before. "I need to think about it."

"Think away. I'm not going anywhere.

Meanwhile, I figure we can get started on the whole getting to know each other better in a non-Biblical sense over dinner. You did promise to feed me."

How did he do that? Say just the right thing to put her back on even keel? Feeling more at ease, she set the beer aside. "So I did. How do you feel about ultimate nachos?"

"I have no idea what your idea of ultimate nachos entails, but I am amenable to nachos of every conceivable type."

"Good." Tugging open the fridge again, she began pulling out ingredients. "There's just one more thing."

"What's that?"

Rowan waited 'til those deep brown eyes met hers. "I'm going to want you to touch me again."

The instant flare of heat in his eyes was gratifying. "I can definitely handle that."

She was counting on it.

~

Nᴀꜱʜ ʟɪꜰᴛᴇᴅ ᴀ ʟᴏᴀᴅᴇᴅ ᴄʜɪᴘ, breaking the string of gooey cheese and wrapping it around the rest of the mountain of toppings. Rowan Beale absolutely had the market cornered on killer nachos. "Now explain to me exactly how you and Robert are related."

"Great niece. My grandfather—mom's dad— is his elder brother. Robert was the oops baby of their generation. Granddad was sixteen when he was born."

"So, he was sort of a big brother uncle to your mom?"

"Exactly. I love my grandfather, but it was always Robert I was closest to. We are, as they say, cut from the same cloth."

"Down to the same profession." Nash tried to picture her in uniform, with her hair all bound up and a tough-girl stare. He liked this relaxed version of her better, barefoot in jeans, with her hair still a little mussed from his hands.

"I used to do ride-alongs with him when I came to visit in the summers. He taught me to shoot, how to do takedowns when I was thirteen and getting harassed in school. He's the reason I became a cop."

"Me, too. Part-time anyway."

"Yeah, how exactly does a pilot end up being a reserve officer?" She shoved a chip in her mouth, then licked the guacamole off her fingers. He couldn't seem to pull his gaze away from the dart of her tongue.

What were they talking about again? Oh, right.

"I was at loose ends when I got out of the Navy. I managed to scrape together enough money to buy Diana, but it takes some time to build up business as a private pilot. Especially since I had no interest in living somewhere big like Atlanta. With my military training, Robert thought law enforcement would be a natural fit, and he convinced me to get the training as a reserve officer to see if I liked it. And I did. But not enough to give up flying. It worked out that I started getting some business as a pilot about the time I finished training, and between the two, I make a comfortable enough living and get to keep doing what I love."

"There's something to be said for carving out your own niche. Will you stick with it, now that Robert's not Chief of Police anymore?"

"Yeah. I've been working more regularly with Wishful PD since his first heart attack because they moved Judd Hamilton up as interim Chief. Now that he's stepped down and moved over to the Sheriff's Department as an investigator, everybody's trying to get a feel for the new guy, Ethan Greer. He's only been here a few weeks, but he seems like a solid cop. Came from the Marshal Service, out of their Dallas office."

"I can't imagine how hard that's been for Robert. I mean, I know he'd been making noises about retirement, but he wanted to do it on his own terms, you know?"

"He likes Ethan, so that helps." Nash pointed at the last chip between them.

Rowan waved at it and sank back in her

chair. "Go right ahead. I think I just ate enough for a week."

Nash popped it into his mouth and washed it down with the last of his beer. "You know, there's still a full-time position vacant in the Wishful PD since Judd left." At her raised brows, he shrugged. "I'm just sayin'. You decide you're sick of big city policing and all those crowds, there's an option. You'd be close to Robert, get some more of that peace and quiet you've been enjoying the last few days. Plus, there's the bonus of my pretty face."

Instead of responding to his flirtatious grin as he'd expected, her blue eyes shuttered, and she tipped back her beer. "I'll keep that in mind."

Too much, too fast, he decided. He'd pushed Rowan far enough tonight. "Well, you said the old man is coming home tomorrow. I should probably get out of your hair so you can finish up whatever needs finishing."

"I'll get the last of those clothes put away, then we're ready to go."

They both rose, working in tandem to clear away the dishes and clean up the mess. Then Rowan walked him to the door.

He paused in the entryway. "Thanks for dinner."

"Thanks for help with The Chair."

"Oh, I think you've already more than thanked me for that."

She huffed a laugh. "Were you always this much of an incorrigible flirt?"

"No. As a teenager I was afraid of girls. As an adult, I find it separates out the women who can take a joke. If they're offended by that kind of behavior, we don't stand a chance, and it's not worth wasting my time. If they've got a sense of humor, then there's something worth exploring."

"Then I guess I have a sense of humor."

He chucked her under the chin. "See? I knew you were a smart woman." Because he knew she expected a toe-curling goodnight kiss, and because he figured he'd pressed his luck enough tonight, Nash brushed a soft kiss to her brow and stepped back.

Rowan narrowed her eyes slightly. "You're just full of surprises."

"Life's more interesting that way. See you tomorrow?"

"Yeah. If you're not busy, you want to ride to Lawley with me to get him?"

"Love to. Night, Rowan."

She stood in the open doorway, watching him as he trotted down the steps and past Robert's truck. Feeling buzzed on more than the single beer and wanting a last look at her, Nash turned back. But the flirty comment died on his lips as he caught sight of something along the side of the truck.

"What the hell?"

On the porch, Rowan straightened. "What is it?"

Nash pulled the phone from his pocket and swiped on the flashlight. Bright red paint stood in garish relief against the white of the pickup. "Somebody's sprayed graffiti on Robert's truck."

"What?" Rowan flew off the porch, crossing the grass in her bare feet until she stood beside him. Then she swore, long and low, her hands curling to fists.

Nash reached out a finger and tested the paint. "Still tacky. Somebody did this while we were inside having dinner."

She spun in a circle, scanning the surrounding woods.

"Whoever did it is probably long gone."

"I didn't hear an engine. I didn't hear anything." She cursed again and turned back to the truck.

Nash panned the light, trying to decipher the image. "Whoever it was has zero artistic talent for tagging. I can't even tell what that's supposed to be."

"It's a whistle."

He angled his head. Yeah, okay, he could sort of, kinda see the Looney Toons style whistle in all the scribbles. "Why the hell would somebody spray paint a whistle on Robert's truck?"

"It's not a message for him. It's a message for me."

"You? Why? What does it mean?"

Her lips pressed into a grim line. "Whistle-blower. Because that's exactly what I am."

CHAPTER 4

It galled Rowan to have to sit back and let someone else work the scene. This...taint from her life in Houston had followed her to Wishful and touched on someone she cared about. Robert didn't need the stress of worrying about all this shit. There was a reason she hadn't told him any of it. She didn't know how she was going to hide it now.

Chief Greer had come himself when Nash made the call to report the vandalism. He came to join her on the porch. Rowan knew before he ever opened his mouth that they hadn't found anything.

"Let me guess—no fingerprints, no tracks, no signs of tampering other than the graffiti itself. You've got no leads on who this might have been or where they might have gone."

"Not right off, no. I need to ask you some questions. Can we go inside where it's a mite warmer?"

"Sure." Only once they'd settled in the kitchen and Nash started puttering around to make coffee did Rowan realize she was chilled through.

"Nash mentioned that you think the message is for you? Have you had trouble with anyone before this?"

She gave a bitter laugh. "I've had plenty of trouble in my own department, but I didn't expect it to follow me here."

"What kind of trouble?"

Rowan hadn't talked about this with anyone outside the department. She didn't know who to trust anymore. But this was Wishful. Her being here was a total fluke, so the likelihood of these men being involved was next to nil.

"At the end of September, my partner and I took a call about a warehouse break-in. By the time we realized it wasn't a simple burglary in progress, the whole thing went sideways. We got pinned down between members of two rival gangs. Reyes was shot and killed. I took a blow to the head. I was in and out of consciousness, and during one of my wakeups I heard a veteran member of our department arguing with the gang leader."

"Heard, not saw?" Ethan prompted.

"Yeah. I was blindfolded. But I knew it was him. He has this very distinctive voice. Bronx meets southern, with a little vocal tick. Anyway, it was obvious he was working with the gang and pissed that they hadn't already killed me. I passed out again, and next time I woke up, the whole place was in the middle of a raid. DEA, Marshals, local SWAT. I owe that team my life."

Nash passed her a mug and squeezed her shoulder. There was no sign of the easygoing flyboy now. The grim set of his jaw reminded her that he'd once been a soldier.

"During debriefing, I reported what I'd heard. None of them had any evidence to support my claims, but they got up with Internal Affairs in my department to start an investigation. Those sorts of things are supposed to be confidential, but it leaked that I was the source who'd made the accusations. I've been getting harassed ever since."

Ethan scribbled notes onto a pad. "I'll contact your department in the morning."

"Don't bother. They don't believe me about the harassment. Or, at the very least, they're looking the other way because they figure I deserve it."

"You didn't report it?"

Rowan bristled. "Of course, I reported it. Or tried. But the evidence had a habit of disappearing."

"Disappearing how?" Nash asked.

"Messages painted on my car window, gone by the time I got back with somebody to document it. A doll with its mouth sewn shut left in my locker, again, gone by the time I got someone willing to come look. After the third time that happened, I started documenting myself before going to get anyone, but..." She shrugged. They could draw their own conclusions without her having to spell out the rest.

Nash tapped his fingers against his mug. "It sounds like somebody's trying to gaslight you."

There was relief in hearing someone else say it. In laying it out and having someone else come to the same conclusion.

"Yeah, well, it worked. At this point, my credibility is shit. I made potential career-ending accusations against a veteran member of the department—accusations that, I might add, have not yet been substantiated by IA. At best, I'm the crazy chick with the head injury, who's got some kind of PTSD after watching her partner die and wants someone in the department to blame. At worst, I'm making it all up to try to garner sympathy."

"Okay, no contacting your department,"

Ethan agreed. "I'll do whatever I can to take care of things here. If someone followed you with intent to continue to harass you while you're here, then chances are they'll try again."

"We could go low-tech and set up a couple of wildlife cameras around the house," Nash suggested. "Hide them well enough and nobody'd know they were there. We might get lucky."

Rowan rubbed at her temples. "Yeah, that's a good idea. And it's something we can do that's low key that Robert probably won't notice. I don't want him knowing about this. He'd be upset, and I'm not going to do anything to stress him out in his condition."

"Understood."

"I've got a buddy who owns a body shop," Nash offered. "I can make arrangements for him to pick it up and get it repainted tomorrow so Robert doesn't see the damage."

He was just racking up all kinds of points tonight. "And if he asks where his truck is?"

"You're having it detailed for him. I'll drive

you to go get him. Then you're not on your own."

Not on your own. The words sent a shaft of…something through her. She'd been so painfully alone since David's death. She hadn't even realized how much she'd been aching for someone, anyone to trust. And here Nash Brewer was with a plan. As she didn't have a better one, Rowan nodded. "Okay."

Ethan rose and offered his hand. "Keep me posted. If you see anything suspicious, hear anything that worries you, give me a call."

She reached out to take it and bobbled her coffee, spilling it across the table and into her lap. "Shit."

"I've got it." Nash sprang into action, bringing back some kitchen towels to mop up the spill.

"Thanks. And thank you for coming out, Chief. I appreciate your personal attention to this."

"I may be new, but it's still my town. I'll be in touch."

They saw him out.

"Why don't you go change into something not covered in coffee," Nash suggested. "I'll toss these towels in the washer."

"You're just full of good ideas tonight."

"Hang on to that thought. I've got a few more."

"Back in a minute." In the guest room, she stripped out of her jeans and t-shirt, and opted for pajama pants and yet another t-shirt. If Nash hadn't been run off by the story of what she'd been through, he could probably stand up to her in comfy clothes.

"Rowan." His voice echoed down the hall.

"Hang on, I'll throw these in that load." Bundling the clothes in a wad, she joined him in the hall.

He stood in front of the washer, something navy in his hands.

"What is it?"

"Is this yours?" He held up what she recognized as her Houston Astros hoodie.

Rowan frowned. "I don't remember pulling that out of my bag."

Nash lifted the sleeve and pointed to the splash of red on the cuff. "It's got the same paint from the truck."

The bottom fell out of her stomach. "Where did you find that?"

"In the washer."

"I didn't do this." Even she heard the thread of desperation in her tone as she lifted her eyes to his. Would he believe her?

"I know you didn't. You were never out of my sight for more than a few minutes at a time. I walked over tonight. It's possible that whoever did this didn't know I was here and didn't count on you having an alibi during the time in question."

He believed her. Without question. Relief made her shake.

"Oh baby." Nash dropped the hoodie and wrapped his arms around her. "You haven't had any allies in this, have you?"

"No." Because it felt so good, she let herself lean, for just a minute. "Nash, whoever did this has been in the house." If the truck had been vandalized during dinner, that meant someone had come in sometime between then and when Ethan had left. That was both ballsy and terrifying.

"Yeah, I thought of that."

They checked for signs of forced entry, inspecting doors and windows, looking for tracks, but as expected, there were none.

"Tomorrow we pick up those cameras on the way to the hospital. I can get them set up and do the monitoring from my place. That way Robert doesn't have to know."

"Okay, good. That's good." Rowan scrubbed a hand over her face. "Thank you for being here, for believing me."

"Of course." He stroked a thumb over her cheek. "You've been through the wringer. Get some sleep. We'll talk about it more in the morning."

She nodded again, starting to feel like a bobblehead doll. But it was so wonderful to have someone else to help, to make some of the decisions.

"I'll sleep in The Chair."

"You what?"

"You're not staying here alone tonight." His tone brooked no argument.

In no mood to argue, and more grateful than she could say, Rowan squeezed his hand. "I'll get you a pillow and blanket."

AT THE BLOOD-CURDLING SCREAM, Nash bolted upright, promptly crashing to the floor in the dark. For a few seconds, he didn't remember where he was or what was going on, but he scrambled to his feet, lifting his hands in a defensive position and listening. Had he dreamed it?

"No!"

Rowan.

Nash ran for the hall, his bare feet slipping on the hardwood floor. She was still screaming as he burst through the bedroom door. But there was no shadowy figure crouched over her on the bed, no man fleeing through an open window or hiding in a corner. There was only Rowan, thrashing in the covers.

Nightmare.

Shifting gears, Nash circled the bed, grabbing at her flailing arms to try and shake her awake. She lashed out, a fist catching him against the temple.

"Ow, shit. Rowan. Rowan, wake up. It's me, Nash." When she only continued to thrash, he used his body weight to pin her. "Wake up!"

She sucked in a lungful of air, and he thought she might scream again, right in his ear. "Nash?"

The fear in her voice shredded his guts. "Yeah, it's me. It's okay. You're safe. You were having a nightmare."

"Off. Off!" Panic drenched her tone.

He backed off, way off, letting her go, though every instinct shouted to hold her. As soon as she was free of his grip, she scuttled away from him, until her back pressed against the wall. Her breath came too fast, too shallow, and her eyes showed white in the dark.

"I'm gonna turn on the light now." He clicked on the lamp at the lowest setting.

Her skin was slicked with sweat, and she was shaking. Nash took a step toward her.

"Don't." The word lashed out like a whip, effectively holding him back.

He curled his hands to fists to keep from reaching for her. She was fucking terrified and didn't want to be touched. What was she dreaming of? Or was she remembering?

Her breath sawed in and out, as if her very throat was sandpaper rough. After the screaming, it probably was.

"You need to slow your breathing down or you'll hyperventilate." Nash perched on the edge of the chair and kept his eyes fixed on hers. "Come on. Slow it down now. In through the nose, out through the mouth."

It took a few minutes. The only sounds in the room were her ragged breath and the faintest ticking from his watch. As each inhale grew deeper, Rowan drew her knees to her chest, wrapping her arms around them and dropping her head. Her whole body trembled.

"Did I say anything?"

"Just 'no.' Nothing more specific."

She made a motion that might have been a nod. It was hard to tell with her curled up in a ball.

"Rowan—"

"Could you get me some water?"

"Yeah, sure. I'll be right back." He wondered if she'd take some hot tea. That's what his mom always used to do when he woke up from a bad dream. Somehow, it seemed an ineffectual response to...whatever that had been.

In the kitchen Nash put ice in a glass and filled it from the tap. As he caught sight of the table, he remembered what she'd told them during her report. The gang members who'd shot her partner hadn't killed her immediately. Which meant they'd either intended to use her for some kind of leverage or they'd had more nefarious uses for her because she was a woman.

She didn't want to be touched. Oh Christ. Had they raped her?

Now he was the one who needed a minute to get his own rage under control. When he was sure he didn't look like he was ready to commit murder, he took the water to her. She hadn't moved from the corner, but her breathing was steadier.

She unfolded enough to take the glass. "I'm sorry. When I agreed you could stay, I didn't think about...this."

"It's a recurring nightmare?"

"Yes. I haven't had it in nearly two weeks, definitely not since I got here. I thought maybe I was past it. I guess with the vandalism and having to go through everything again with Chief Greer, it all got stirred up again."

"The night your partner died."

"Yes." She sipped at the water. "I just keep seeing it, stuck on a loop. Every time, I try to do something to stop it, to change it. Every time, I fail, and David ends up dead." Tears spilled over, sliding down her pale cheeks.

Nash couldn't take it anymore, he moved to the edge of the bed. "I won't touch you if you don't want me to, but I just—tell me what I can do."

"I'm not the cry on your shoulder type."

"Is that natural inclination or did something else happen to you that night?"

Rowan frowned. "What do you mean?"

Should he just come right out and say it? No, even he wasn't that blunt. "Did they do more than beat you?"

Realization slid over her face. "They didn't sexually assault me, no. I expect they would have, if they'd had me long enough, but I was spared that, at least."

Nash loosed a breath of his own and sat on the bed, feeling some of the tension bleed out. "Good. So why the distance? Because it's taking everything I have not to just haul you into my lap to comfort you."

"I'm not good with weakness."

"Everybody's got weaknesses."

"Yeah, but I'm a woman in what most people still see as a man's job. Any hint of softness or vulnerability is something I can get crucified for."

"You're not at work, Rowan. And I'm sure as shit not judging you for having a very human response to a beyond shitty situation. I've been to war. I've seen friends and enemies killed in battle. That shit sticks with you. The only way you really survive it is to let somebody else in. I'm not saying it has to be me—I realize we don't know each other that well yet—but it needs to be somebody. Because it'll eat you alive."

She watched him with those sad blue eyes for a long moment, then slowly stretched out a hand across the bed. Nash took it without hesitation. It wasn't what he wanted, but it was a step, and maybe for tonight, that was enough.

CHAPTER 5

"I don't know why you thought you had to go getting my truck detailed."

Rowan opened the back passenger door to Nash's truck. "It's called a nice gesture, old man. Besides, you can't drive it yourself for a while, so what are you grumping about?" She hoped the usual ribbing would distract him from asking any more questions. She'd been inordinately nervous all day, expecting to be busted like a teenager who'd snuck out after curfew.

Not even Nash's usually calming influence did much to unravel the knots in her belly. Subterfuge wasn't something she'd ever been comfortable with.

He harrumphed and ignored the hand she offered to help him out. Sliding out of the seat, his cheeks went white, and his jaw tensed. Rowan automatically reached to steady him, but the furious glare he shot in her direction stayed her hand. Still, she hovered as he made his way toward the steps. There were only three, but the doctor had warned them that steps might be difficult for a while.

Rowan exchanged a Look with Nash as Robert hesitated at the base. If either of them tried to help him, they'd get snapped at. Nash edged closer, obviously ready to jump in if needed. But Robert made it. He had to rest for a full minute between steps, but he made it. So, they said nothing, only trailed him up the stairs.

Rowan unlocked the house, bracing herself for an explosion over the changes she'd made while he'd been hospitalized. "I got you a present." She fisted her hand to keep from trying to take his arm as he stepped over the threshold, into the living room.

Robert stopped and huffed again. "An old-man chair. Some present."

"Man, if you don't want it, I do," Nash put in. "That right there is the Cadillac of recliners. Perfect for a Saturday afternoon watching football—one of the games for your second-string team that you don't mind falling asleep during."

"Why don't you at least give it a try?" Rowan suggested, aiming for a conciliatory tone.

Robert shot her a dark look. "I sit in that thing, I'm not likely to be able to get back out."

"You'll just have to be careful, is all. The doctor recommended a recliner."

Instead of sitting, he went into the kitchen.

Nash dropped his voice. "If you can keep him distracted, I can get the cameras in place. I finished all the setup while you were dealing with discharge."

"Go," she whispered.

In the kitchen, Robert stood in front of the open refrigerator. "What the hell is this?"

Rowan peered past him. "Low-fat yogurt. Fresh vegetables. And the salmon filet I was planning on cooking for dinner tonight."

"I'm out of the hospital. I expected to get real food."

"This is real food, Unk."

"Rabbit food, maybe." Disgusted, he shut the door. Rowan thought he might head down the hall to his room, but he pulled out a chair and sat at the kitchen table.

She didn't like how heavy he was breathing.

"Quit looking at me like I'm gonna keel over. I'm fine," he snapped.

And suddenly it was too much. All the stress and worry about him boiled over. "You're not fine," Rowan barked. "You just had bypass surgery, and I'm allowed to be freaked the hell out about that. I thought I'd lost you. Do you have any idea what that would do to me? You are the only member of this family who truly gets me, and I love you. So, for better or worse, you are going to have to get the hell over this shit attitude because I'm here to make sure you follow the doctor's orders to the letter this time so that you don't keel over again. Got it?"

Robert narrowed his eyes. "I'm a shit patient."

"We have established this. Here, have some water." She grabbed a bottle from the fridge and twisted off the cap. "I don't care that you're a shit patient. I care that you get better. And I'm staying until I know you are, so get used to it."

He took a long pull on the water, blue eyes sharp on her. "How can you stick around taking care of me, anyway?"

"I have the leave time. I'm taking it. You're important." It was the absolute truth, even if it wasn't the *whole* truth.

He saw through her bravado. "How have you been doing at work since Reyes?"

Rowan didn't want to lie to him. "My captain and the department shrink thought I could

WATCH OVER ME | 73

use some time to decompress, away from things." She jerked her shoulders and opened the fridge to see what she could throw together for their lunch. "I admit they were right, to some extent. Being here in Wishful has been good." Despite the vandalism of his truck. But she wasn't going to mention that. "I never imagined I'd be one for calm and quiet, but it's growing on me."

"You could always stay."

Considering his attitude today, the remark surprised her. "You've been wanting to get rid of me since I walked through the hospital doors this morning."

"I don't want a keeper. Doesn't mean I wouldn't enjoy having you around more often. With all the changes in the department here since my first heart attack, there's a hole in the ranks they haven't gotten around to filling yet."

Nash had mentioned the same, and it was tempting. Just start over in a new town, with new people. Away from all the stress and the reminders of her partner. But that felt too much like running away from the problem. Her department had serious problems, problems that she was starting to believe had resulted in David's death. Someone had to put a stop to it. She'd never be able to forgive herself if she didn't follow through.

But there was a part of her that remembered her reaction to the nightmare last night. She'd thought she was getting better, but that bout had been almost as bad as the days right after it happened. Was she actually fit for duty right now?

It had been worse, somehow, seeing Nash's response. When it was just her, she could mini-mize the whole thing, talk herself down. But there was no escaping that he'd been legiti-mately worried. Quite apart from the fact that she'd scared the hell out of him with her screaming, he'd been wound almost as tight as she was, worried he'd say or do the wrong thing. He'd needed to comfort, and it had taken everything she had not to just crawl into his arms and stay there the rest of the night. But she viewed that the same way she viewed alcohol. A prospective crutch.

It was one thing to explore the chemistry between them, to let him distract her while she was here—if that was still on the table after last night. It was quite another to let him in at her most vulnerable. Because her time here was temporary.

Realizing Robert was still staring at her, Rowan finished slapping some turkey between two slices of whole grain bread and spread a thin layer of Miracle Whip over the whole thing. "I've got a job, Unk. And for now, that's taking care of you."

WHEN NASH OPENED his door to Rowan a week later, he took one look at her and asked, "Beer, hug, or chocolate?"

She winced. "All three?"

Poor baby. "That I can do." He pulled her in, liking that she hesitated only a moment before resting her head against his chest. He wanted to get his mouth on her again, but that wasn't what she needed just now, so he kept things G-rated and rubbed slow circles on the small of her back. "How's our patient?"

"Cranky. Oh my God, so cranky. He's worse than my partner's toddler when she doesn't get a nap. Not that I blame him. If I had to give up fat and salt, and wasn't allowed to do anything, I'd be cranky, too. I made turkey burgers for dinner last night, and I thought he was going to throw it against the wall."

Nash leaned back far enough to look down at her. "You haven't tried shoving the heinousness of turkey bacon on him, have you? Because that shit is a crime against food."

"Do I look suicidal?" She stepped away and eyed him. "Do you really have chocolate?"

"Well, technically, it's chocolate with peanut butter. I've got those Reese's Christmas trees."

Longing flitted over her face. "You are a god among men."

Laughing, he grabbed her hand and towed

her back to the kitchen. "C'mon. We'll get movie snacks before we sit down with the camera footage. How's Chief Grumpy doing otherwise?"

"A little better. Jonesing to do more than he is. The incision is healing well, and he hasn't had any signs of infection. But I think he expected to be further along after a week out of the hospital."

Retrieving the candy, he changed directions and headed for the living room. Rowan made no move to tug her hand free, and that pleased Nash enormously. He hadn't been happy to hold a girl's hand since high school. They sat on the sofa, in front of the laptop he'd hooked up to the TV on the wall.

"I assume, since you haven't mentioned anything, that everything's been quiet?"

"Nary a peep. If it was someone from my home department, maybe it was a one and done and they headed home. It's not like most people have the vacation to burn to just hang out here and harass me."

"Could be," Nash agreed. But he felt better they had eyes on the house. Hitting a few keys, he brought up the program that managed the cameras.

"How many hours of footage do we have?"

"It's not that bad. They don't run continuously. There's a motion detector. If something moves, then it kicks on." He checked the status. "Looks like one of them went down sometime last night. Might need to check the batteries in that one, but we'll watch the footage first." A few more keystrokes, and both feeds filled the screen.

They sat back, unwrapping the candy and noshing as they watched the local wildlife parade by. Deer. A fox. Several raccoons. A possum. Even an armadillo.

Rowan sat forward. "Wait, look. The door just opened. Jesus, someone's been in the house! Slow it down."

Nash did as she asked. The dark figure slipped out of the front door and moved with a shuffling gait down the steps. "That's weird. It's like he doesn't know what he's doing or where he's going. There's no effort at stealth at all."

"I think it's a woman. Look, small stature."

"Yeah, I think you're right."

They watched as the woman neared the camera. Rowan's hand tightened on his, and they both held their breath, waiting to see if they'd get a face.

The angle was terrible, but she walked right up to the camera, close enough to catch the vacant expression and unfocused eyes before she reached out toward the camera and the screen went black.

"What the hell? It's…"

"Me," Rowan said. "I don't understand. I didn't go outside last night. Except, obviously, I did."

"It looked like you were sleepwalking. Do you have a history of that?"

She shook her head. "Not since I was a little bitty kid. I haven't sleepwalked in years."

"That you know of."

"What do you mean?"

"Have you been sharing your bed with anybody in the past few months who could verify? Sleepwalking can be aggravated by stress. You've been under plenty. It could be you have been and ended up back in your bed by morning, not to be any wiser. I had a guy in my unit who'd wander all the way down to the mess hall and sleep eat. He'd still be back in bed by PT."

Unease rippled over her face, and she released his hand, reaching for more chocolate. "Sleepwalking always freaked me out as a concept. I mean, what's to stop you from walking into traffic? Sleep...anything seems like a bad, bad idea in the household of a cop with guns."

Given her nightmares, that *was* a terrifying concept. "Fair point. But you weren't armed, and Robert keeps his weapons in a gun safe."

Nash considered what he knew of the situation, going over the night of the vandalism in his head. "That night I came over for dinner, before Robert came home, I walked up to the house on the opposite side of the truck. The paint could've been there and I wouldn't even have noticed." Rowan frowned, but he continued. "There was paint on your hoodie. If you're sleepwalking, you could've done it yourself and not even known."

She angled toward him, but somehow, it felt like she'd put a mile between them. "So, you think I'm crazy." The tough girl mask was in place, but Nash could see the fear beneath. This was so clearly her fear. And why shouldn't it be, under the circumstances?

"I think you're stressed. And understandably so. Could any of the other harassment you experienced have been something that happened while you were sleeping?"

Her answer was a quick, vehement shake of her head. "No." But she didn't quite meet his eyes as she said it.

Not wanting to alienate her or to make her feel like he was against her too, Nash let it drop. "Okay. It was just a thought. We'll get that camera back up and running properly to keep an eye on things. Meanwhile, maybe we should set up feeders to draw in some more of the wildlife. It might help alleviate Chief Grumpy's boredom."

Her lips twitched faintly. "Don't let him hear you call him that."

"If the shoe fits, darlin'. If the shoe fits."

CHAPTER 6

"*H*as there been a woman in here… ever?" Rowan eyed the warehouse that was Blanchard's Boxing Gym. The place was minimalist in the extreme. Racks of free weights lined one wall, beside a power rack and a Smith machine. Another huge frame held a row of heavy bags. Beside that was a station with heavy, nautical-style ropes. An enormous tractor tire leaned against the wall. Half the floor was covered in blue mats, and a classic raised boxing ring dominated the far end. A cushy, cardio palace it was not. It immediately made her homesick for her gym in Houston, which was the big brother of this one, a place frequented by cops, firefighters, and military types.

"There are women who come here," Nash defended. "It's just not geared toward the kind of fitness most of them go for. Reuben's got a Crossfit class that's pretty popular with the ladies.

Rowan's interest piqued at that. If she ended up staying longer than expected, she'd definitely have to check that out. As it was, she'd been making do with bodyweight workouts in her room. It wasn't enough to curb the growing restlessness or to distract her from the theory Nash had raised the other night, but Robert wasn't where she could leave him alone yet. She'd only managed to steal an hour or two away today because one of his fishing buddies had stopped by to shoot the shit. Thank God. She'd been going stir crazy cooped up in the house with Chief Grumpy.

"Brewer! You here for a rematch?" A big, bald tank of a man lifted a gloved hand in the boxing ring.

Nash lifted his in return. "C'mon, there are some folks I want you to meet."

She trailed him over to the ring.

"Y'all, this is Rowan Beale, Robert's great niece. She's in town keeping an eye on him since his heart attack. Rowan, this is Reuben Blanchard. This is his gym."

Rowan offered her hand and found it engulfed in a much larger one. "Nice place you've got here."

A grin split his dark face. "It's no frills, but it does the job."

"You were one of my uncle's reserve officers, weren't you? Former SEAL?"

"Yes ma'am, I am. And you're with Houston PD."

"I am." Why did that feel like a lie? Despite everything that had happened, she was still with the department.

"This here is Clint Yarbrough, another

Wishful PD officer who worked with Chief Curry."

Clint's handshake was firm. "Chief talked a lot about you. How's he doing?"

"We've come close to killing each other four or five times. He hates being sidelined, and neither of us is used to this much...confinement. But his two-week follow-up is tomorrow, so we're hopeful his doctor will clear him for more activity."

"I expect he's bellyaching like a stuck pig," Reuben observed, dark eyes glittering with amusement.

Rowan laughed. "Oh, you have no idea."

"Since she had a couple hours, I figured I'd bring her down here to blow off some steam," Nash said.

"I may be a bit rusty," Rowan warned. "But then, since you volunteered your own ass for kicking, maybe you're counting on that."

Nash pulled a face. "Me? I would never cast such aspersions."

Rowan snorted. "Stretch out, Flyboy. Let's see what you've got."

"You wanna borrow some pads?" Nash asked. "There are bound to be some floating around somewhere that will do."

"Last time I checked, perps don't wait for you to put on additional safety gear before attacking." But she strode over to the bins of athletic tape and pre-wrap to protect her knuckles.

By the time they'd both limbered up, Reuben and Clint had finished their match and vacated the ring. Nash made an after-you gesture. Rowan would've preferred the mats, but at this point, she'd already accepted that every man in there would be watching them. Who could blame them? Nash had a good six inches and fifty pounds on her. Probably they all assumed he'd go easy on the little woman. Let him. After she'd knocked him on his ass a few times, maybe things would actually get interesting.

Ducking beneath the lower rope, Rowan

rolled into the ring and to her feet. They met at the center, shook hands, then broke into fighting stances. Nash was taller, with a much longer reach. Rowan danced forward and back, dodging as he feinted. He didn't want to really hit her. His mistake. On his next punch, she slipped under his guard, landing a solid side kick to his gut that made his breath whoosh out with a satisfying *ooph*.

One hand dropped to protect his belly. "We're using feet?"

"We didn't establish rules, so anything goes."

It felt good to move, good to feel the prick of sweat at her temple. So much of the past few months had been on the defensive. It felt better to be on active offense. To channel some of this frustration and rage into physical activity. She thought about every criticism, every doubt she'd faced since David died. And she thought of the concern in Nash's eyes as he'd suggested she'd sleepwalked all the harassment herself. She shot like a bullet beneath his guard, pistoning rabbit punches to his ribs and driving him back against the ropes.

Rowan felt it the moment he stopped taking it easy on her. His stance shifted, and he shoved her hard enough to knock her off balance, have her stumbling back. But instead of landing on her ass, she rolled, coming neatly to her feet and diving at him again, feet and fists whirling. He blocked, and the impact of it sang up her arm. Some of the temper bled off. How could she stay mad at him for pointing out the obvious possible solution? They had incontrovertible proof that she *was* sleepwalking again. A small part of her actually relished the idea that this was all in her head. If that were true, then she didn't have to worry about external dangers on top of Robert's condition. She didn't have to believe that any of the men and women she'd been working with all these years, who she'd trusted to have her back, were corrupt.

But if it was all in her head, then was she even competent? Discomfort slithered through her at the notion. All she'd ever wanted was to be a cop. To protect and defend. If she couldn't do that, who was she?

Wanting to prove something—to herself, if not to anyone else—Rowan dialed it up to eleven, pulling no punches, and hitting Nash with everything she had. Sweat streamed down her face and her breath came in pants. When he took her to the floor with a tackle around her middle, she landed hard, losing her breath and the upper hand. She realized as he loomed over her—grinning, damn him—using his bigger bulk to pin her, that she wasn't angry with him anymore. But she wasn't ready to call uncle yet.

"That all you got, Flyboy?"

"Loco."

"What?"

"My nickname was Loco. And I'd say I've got the control at the moment." He bracketed her wrists with his hands, pinning them to the mat above her head.

The position thrust her breasts against his chest, and she had a flashback to The Chair and that crazy make-out session. And suddenly this sparring match felt a whole lot less like blowing off steam and more like a good way to generate some. Rowan sucked in a breath, watching his pupils dilate. She licked her lips, and his gaze dropped to her mouth. Taking advantage of his distraction, she bridged and rolled, tossing him off her and scrambling to get an arm bar. Finding it, she cranked back.

Laughing, Nash tapped out. "Okay. I call uncle."

Winded, Rowan released him and flopped back on the mat as their small audience whooped and cheered. Her muscles were worn and loose, and she felt more relaxed than she had in months. Here, in this tiny town, with this particular man, she didn't have to keep her guard up. She could breathe. Turning her head, she shot him a smile. "That was *fun*. Thanks. It was just what I needed."

"You're good."

"I ought to be after two black belts." Not that they'd helped when she and David had been taking fire.

Nash rolled to his knees and shoved to his feet. "Come out with me tomorrow."

That effectively pulled her away from dark thoughts. "What?"

He tugged her to her feet, steadying her as her body bumped into his. "Come out with me."

"Like a date?"

"Not *like* a date. An actual date. We both know Robert's gonna get cleared. You need a night out, and he needs a night of quiet. Come out with me."

His easygoing manner was such a temptation. Hell, everything about him was temptation. And she'd be lying if she didn't admit she wanted his mouth on hers again. "Okay, Flyboy, it's a date."

WHEN NASH HAD ASKED Rowan out yesterday, he hadn't been thinking beyond wanting to spend more time with her and unraveling all those knots of tension she seemed to tote around like Marley's chains. Well, and kissing her again. But as he backed his truck out of his own driveway and whipped around to pull it into Robert's, it occurred to him that it wasn't just Rowan he needed to impress tonight. He had no idea how Robert would react to this.

They were friends. Robert had been a sort of mentor since Nash had separated from the Navy. But Rowan was something else entirely. Despite their headbutting the last couple of weeks, the two shared a bond far more like father and daughter. And that made Nash nervous.

He was never nervous.

He'd opted for low-key—a diner or Mexican food kinda date. Not that he didn't think Rowan would appreciate a fancy dinner at Tosca or out at The Spring House, but those all seemed to add additional pressure to an outing he hoped would take her mind off things. Plus, she'd packed in a hurry to come to Wishful to play nursemaid. He doubted she'd included any kind of dressy clothes. Considering what her ass did for a pair of jeans, Nash had no problem with that. He could rock a suit if he had to, but ninety-nine times out of a hundred, he'd choose not to.

Still, he wondered if Robert would think he'd gone to enough effort. Maybe he should've bought flowers.

Too late now.

He knocked on the door. Rowan answered it a few seconds later, barefoot, in jeans—praise God—and a soft, green, V-neck sweater, one hand sliding a pair of tiny silver hoops in her ears. Pretty much the whole time he'd known her, she'd been very *au naturale*, foregoing makeup. She was beautiful without all the fuss. But it turned out the fuss was appealing, too. She'd done something to her eyes that made them pop and slicked her lips with some kind of gloss that made him wonder if she'd taste like peaches.

"You look great."

The corner of her mouth kicked up. "Thanks. I'll be ready in just a second."

Nash followed her into the living room where Robert sat in The Chair.

"The roasted chicken and carrots are in the fridge, along with a batch of green beans," Rowan said, dropping onto the sofa to pull on her socks and some ankle boots. "You just need to heat them up when you're ready for dinner."

Robert pulled a face.

"And don't you even think about ordering take out. I've already talked to every restaurant in the area who will deliver and warned them not to take orders for you."

Her great uncle appeared deeply unimpressed. Nash stifled a laugh, at least until Robert's attention swung to him.

Those sharp blue eyes skimmed over him, assessing. Rowan's eyes, yet not. It was like being judged by his superior officers, and it took everything he had to stay relaxed and casual rather than coming to attention for inspection.

"Thank you for giving me some peace and quiet."

Rowan stood. "Gee, thanks. I love you, too." She slipped on a coat. "Ready?"

"After you."

"Please, God, don't hurry back," Robert called.

Nash's stride hitched for half a second. He didn't want to think about what Robert might be giving his blessing to because that just felt weird. But he wasn't threatening to string Nash up or greet him with a shotgun. Then again, Rowan was more than capable on her own. Maybe he was overthinking this whole thing.

Once outside, he scooted past her to open the truck door for her. She eyed him but said nothing as she slipped inside. Skirting the hood, Nash climbed into the driver's seat. "What sounds good for dinner? Our options are basically pizza, bar food, Mexican, or the diner."

"I would kill for a good margarita right now."

"Los Pantalones it is." Shoving the truck into gear he backed out and headed for town. "So how did the check-up go? You didn't cancel, so I'm guessing it went well."

"Yeah. He's healing well. They're signing him up for cardiac rehab and, in the meantime, he's allowed to start gradually increasing his daily activity, which should hopefully improve his crap attitude."

"Here's hoping. Meanwhile, further discussion of Robert is off the table the rest of the night. You need to have a few hours of not thinking and worrying about it."

She dropped her head back against the seat with a sigh. "I fully support this plan."

The parking lot was full, as was usually the case on any given night of the week. During their brief wait for a table, they said little. Conversation would've been difficult over the din of the crowd. Nash watched her scan every face. Usual cop threat assessment or was she looking for someone familiar from Houston? In the days since their discovery of her sleepwalking, there'd been no repetition. If she was still doing it, she wasn't being caught on camera.

Had it been a one-time thing or was it an on-going problem? He didn't know and hadn't asked. Other than giving her a daily report from the footage, Nash hadn't brought it up. As she hadn't mentioned any other incidents, he assumed all had been quiet on that front.

The hostess led them through the labyrinth of tables to one in the back. As she sat, accepting a menu, Rowan looked toward the corner. "Is that a Christmas tree with chili pepper lights?"

"Yes. Yes, it is."

She blinked, as if just realizing. "It's Christmas."

"Yeah." Nash chuckled. "Did you miss the notice? Cause they put out Christmas stuff at all the retailers the day after Halloween."

"No, I just—have had other things on my mind. I should decorate. Pick up a tree or something."

"Applewhite Farms always has a tree lot over at McSweeney's Market. Or if you want to pick your own, they do big business out at the actual tree farm. I've never done it, but I'm told they do it up right with wagon rides and mulled cider and stuff."

"It sounds all quaint and small town and...*normal.* I could do with some normal, even if it isn't *my* normal."

"I happen to be excellent at picking the perfect tree, and my mama will tell you I am an expert at putting on lights."

"Are you, now?"

"Oh yes. Mama fancies herself an interior decorator at the holidays, and she has very exacting standards. I'm well-trained."

She smiled and finally seemed to focus in on him, which felt like a victory. "I'll think about it. I don't even know what kind of decorations He Who We Are Not Discussing has. He usually comes to us for Christmas."

"And where does that usually take place? I realize I don't actually know where you're originally from."

"Gulfport. My grandfather and parents are still there."

"You wanna go back?"

"No, I never felt that pull. I wanted to get away from home."

"Why Houston? Are you one of those people who's all into the energy of a city?" Those people were, as far as Nash was concerned, an alien species.

"Not really. And some days the crowds and the traffic really get to me. But there were really good opportunities with the police department there. It's a huge department in a large metropolitan area, so every day tends to be different. And there were a ton of divisions I could ultimately specialize in."

He studied her. "Were?"

"Sorry?"

"You used the past tense."

The automatic way her face shuttered had Nash kicking himself for pointing out the slip. He was grateful the waitress arrived with a basket of chips and to take their orders. Once she'd gone, he was all prepared to redirect the conversation and pretend he hadn't asked, but Rowan spoke before he had the chance.

"I said 'were' because it's highly unlikely I'll ever be promoted within the ranks."

"You're a good cop. That's not an area where Robert would give false praise."

"I'm a good cop who made accusations against a decorated veteran of the force. I've had plenty of time to think about this since I've been here. There's been no break in the case while I was gone, and I'm not foolish enough to believe that attitudes toward me in the department are going to change. Even if my accusations are substantiated eventually, there is a huge subset who will never forgive me for violating the code and turning against one of our own."

"So, you find a new department."

"Even if that were an option—and I don't feel that it is until I see this thing through, for the sake of my partner—law enforcement is a small world. The things I've said, the things I've done, will follow me no matter where I go. I'm either branded a turncoat or a mentally unstable woman who is so damaged by the death of her partner, I'm not actually fit for duty. I've been wrestling with the very real possibility that I've destroyed the career I've worked so hard for."

The gravity of that sank in as the waitress returned with their margaritas and a bowl of cheese dip. Jesus, he hadn't expected the conversation to head in this kind of direction. He'd wanted to help her relax tonight, not drag up all the *other* shit she didn't want to talk about. And what the hell could he say to make her feel better against *that?* He understood the uncertainty associated with switching careers. He hadn't known what he wanted when he left the Navy. But leaving had been his choice, not something forced upon him.

Rowan reached for her drink but didn't lift it from the table. She wrapped her fingers around the cactus stem of the glass and stared into the bowl. Her voice, when she finally spoke, was so quiet, Nash barely heard her. "I don't know who I am if I'm not a cop. It's the only thing I ever wanted to be."

She was a woman who hated vulnerability, avoided letting anyone in. That she'd confide this fear to him left Nash feeling humbled and completely ill-equipped to say or do the right thing. Now wasn't the time for some flip or outrageous remark, and he sure as hell didn't know the right answer. To buy himself some time, he took her hand, lacing their fingers.

"I don't know the answer. And I can't even begin to imagine how hard this is for you. But I do know that you're an honorable woman. You're standing up for what you believe in, honoring your partner's memory. If you'd done anything less, you wouldn't be the cop Robert is so proud of. Maybe you will have to go some-where new, and maybe you don't know where that is—" Nash restrained himself from pushing Wishful again. "But your career isn't over un-less you decide it is. The Rowan I know is not a woman who gives up easily."

He expected her to have some kind of

comeback about how he didn't really know her. Instead, she straightened her shoulders and lifted her glass.

"To keeping the faith. And those who help you do it when it's hard."

Nash tapped his margarita to hers. "Cheers."

CHAPTER 7

"No date in Wishful is complete without a stroll of the town green and over to the fountain," Nash announced.

Rowan hunched into her coat. "That a fact?"

"Absolutely." He swung an arm around her, tugging her into his warmth. It was such a blatant move, she almost laughed. But as the temperatures had dropped considerably during dinner and he seemed to be a walking, talking furnace, she slid an arm around his waist instead.

Despite his proclamation, few people were

out in the cold, night air. This time of night, the only things still open around the green were the diner, The Mudcat Tavern, and Speakeasy Pizza. Their patrons filled about half the available parking spaces downtown, but the sidewalks were mostly empty. The whole place was an idyllic picture out of some Hallmark Channel movie set in the South. Each lamppost was wrapped in garland and Christmas lights, and an enormous Christmas tree towered in front of City Hall. There were even the faint strains of Christmas music floating out from speakers mounted along Main Street. Walking here, with him, it was easy to forget everything going wrong in her life. Nash made it hard to focus on anything but what was going right.

By the side of the fountain, he stopped. "Want to make a wish?"

"Is that part of Wishful dating etiquette, too?"

"It's part of Wishful, period. Don't tell me you've been coming here all these years to visit Robert and you've never made one."

"It may have escaped your notice, but my great uncle is not what you can call a fanciful man. He's not exactly up on the idea of wishes."

Nash pressed a hand to his heart as if the statement pained him. "This is an oversight that must be rectified." Digging into his pocket he pulled out a coin and pressed it into her palm. "Hold it tight in your hand as you formulate your wish, then let her fly."

Rowan wasn't big on the idea of wishes herself. She believed in what she could control. What she could touch and see. The notion of some kind of woo woo attached to the fountain because it was fed from nearby Hope Springs was outside her willingness to suspend disbelief. But saying so in the face of his cheerful earnestness would've been tantamount to kicking a puppy.

As the quarter warmed in her palm, she considered her options. She could wish for answers in the investigation. For this whole situation back in Houston to be over. She could wish for Robert to recover without further problems. She almost, almost went for that. But just as she was about to toss it in, Rowan looked up at Nash.

He was watching her, and while she saw his customary good humor, there was more lingering in the depths of those brown eyes. He didn't look at her like she was broken or crazy. Nothing in his expression made her feel like less. Instead, the blend of affection and simmering heat made her feel wanted and...alive for the first time since David's death. She didn't want that feeling to end.

I wish for Nash to never stop looking at me like he's looking right now.

She tossed the coin, not even glancing over to see where it landed in the water.

Nash smiled, curving his hands around her hips. "There now. That's better."

It certainly was. Though he didn't hold her tight, Rowan could feel each individual finger where it pressed against her, as if they burned through her clothes. She stepped into him, lifting her mouth to brush over his, delighting in the instant flash of heat from him before he dialed it back a notch, presumably for the sake of that handful of people still wandering about. She didn't want that heat dialed back. She wanted it dialed up. She wanted him, and she could no longer think of any good reasons to fight that, especially as the feeling was so obviously mutual.

Dropping back to her feet, she broke the kiss, gripping his arms to steady herself. "Take me home, Nash."

He checked his watch. "You want to go check on Robert? He's probably—"

"Your home."

He blinked once, twice, and then that flash of heat streaked over his face again before settling to a low smolder in his eyes. "Yes, ma'am."

They made it back to his truck in record time. He didn't speak on the drive back. His usual lackadaisical attitude had been replaced with an intensity she found intriguing. Tension built in the cab until it hummed along her skin, and it was so much better than the stress and the grief and the worry.

She glanced once at her great uncle's house as they drove past, grateful Nash's place was set well back from the road. The lights were on. Would he see them drive by? Under ordinary circumstances, she had no doubt Robert would be well aware of the comings and goings of his neighbors. But he wasn't up to his usual observational skills. Or maybe that was wishful thinking. For half a second, she wondered if this was a good idea. Nash and Robert were friends. When she went back to Houston, Nash would still live here. Then they pulled into Nash's garage and put the door down, and she stopped wondering.

Rowan slid out of the truck before he could come around to open the door for her. He took her hand again in the kitchen, and her heart jumped with sudden nerves. As if he sensed it, his thumb brushed over the pulse point in her wrist. Did he feel it thudding against his finger?

"You want anything? A beer? I could maybe scare up a bottle of wine."

"Just you."

His eyes went impossibly darker at her statement, and his fingers tightened around hers. She expected he'd get down to business, maybe pull her over to the sofa or lead her back to his bedroom. Instead, he slowly lifted the hand he held and pressed a kiss to her palm.

Rowan's heart did a slow roll in her chest. "Wh…" Damn it, why was she stuttering? "What are you doing?"

His lips curved as he shifted slightly to kiss the pulse in her wrist. "Seducing you."

Oh God.

She swallowed, suddenly feeling very, very out of her depth.

Nash stepped into her, tipping her chin up with his free hand and brushing his lips over hers in a lazy, somehow claiming kiss that turned her knees to water. Her hands found their way to his waist, gripping at his shirt and then forgetting their task, as he continued that unhurried assault on her mouth, fogging her brain until her discomfort floated away, insubstantial as smoke. He kissed her until her body thrummed. Only then did he touch her, breaking that stillness to slide a wide palm beneath the hem of her sweater to splay against her back. The slightest of pressures had her flowing into him, feeling the press of that long, lean body against hers, moving—but not how she wanted.

Rowan realized dimly that the light had changed. He'd worked them down the hall into a bedroom. It was dark, and she was grateful, as she wasn't wearing anything special. Just a basic cotton bra and panties that didn't even match. She didn't ordinarily care about such things. But the way he kissed her, as if she were something beautiful and precious made her wish she'd taken the time and effort. Then again, she hadn't planned on ending up in his bed when she'd dressed tonight.

A second hand slid beneath her sweater, this one skimming up her torso to palm a breast.

Her nipples went taut even as her toes curled inside her boots. This scenic route exploration of her body was going to drive her insane. Struggling to focus on something besides that sinful mouth of his, Rowan forced her fingers to work, tugging his shirt free and fumbling the buttons open. He gave a gratifying hiss of breath as she laid her hands against the planes of his chest. She explored every inch with her fingers, greedy and impatient, hoping to speed him up. His only answer was to pull her closer, fitting her body to his until the bulge in his jeans pressed against her hips.

Rowan's hands arrowed down, groping for his belt before she lost her temporary dexterity.

He lifted the sweater, effectively staying her hands and trapping her arms as he tugged it up and off. Static buzzed and popped as he pulled it free of her hair, and she could swear she felt it along every inch of newly exposed skin. Or maybe that was the electricity building between them. Rowan nudged off his shirt, pressing skin to skin and lifting to her toes to nibble along the column of his throat. He angled against her mouth, his own hands fumbling with the clasp of her bra. And that was another little victory, even as he took ten times longer than she wanted.

Then her breasts were bare, and he was lifting her, just scooping her up with his hands behind her thighs and sinking onto the bed so she straddled his lap, and he could suck one nipple into his mouth.

"Oh God."

At her breathy moan, he rocked beneath her, the hardness of him rubbing against the heat of her through far too many layers of clothing. She started to say something but lost her train of thought as he shifted to the other breast and worshipped her. There was no other word for it. And it felt glorious. She plowed her fingers into his hair and began to move her hips to the rhythm he set, feeling her body coiling tighter at the delicious friction that wasn't nearly enough.

One hand pinned her hips tighter to his as

the other covered her free breast, rolling the nipple between his fingers as his mouth continued to lick and suck until pleasure shot through her like lightning as she tipped into delicious madness.

Rowan slumped, boneless, in his lap, head dropping weakly to his shoulder. Smug, Nash lifted his mouth from her glorious breasts. She'd come apart so fast, and they weren't even totally naked yet. Points to him.

Then she began to laugh. No, not laugh. That was a straight up, girlish *giggle.*

Okay, not the response he'd expected. "Something funny?"

She combed her fingers through his hair. "You're much, much better at this than any horny, teenage boy." He could hear the grin in her voice.

Laughing himself, Nash rolled until she was beneath him. "I'm about to prove in no uncertain terms that I am definitely not a teenage boy."

She arched her hips against him. "Please do."

He made quick work of the little ankle boots, dropping them with a thud to the floor. Her jeans and panties came next. He took more time with them, kissing each new inch of revealed skin as he tugged them down, down. By the time he finished, he was a little drunk on the musky scent of her arousal and the little sounds of pleasure she made. His own jeans were beyond uncomfortable. But he loved every minute, knowing he could take her out of her own head, away from her problems and stresses, to focus only on him, on how he made her feel.

"Nash."

He paused. "Yeah?"

"You aren't nearly naked enough."

He dropped his jeans and boxers, stepping free. "How 'bout now?"

"Don't know. I think you have to come closer for inspection."

His cock twitched at the idea of that. Crawling back up her body, he stretched over her, stopping a few inches shy of where he really wanted to be. "How 'bout now?"

Even in the ambient light from down the hall, he could see her eyes glitter. She wrapped a hand around him, and his eyes rolled back in his head. "We're getting there." She made a few, testing strokes along his length that had him surging forward in her hand. "Definitely not a teenage boy."

He choked out her name and fought for some control. "I'm trying to take my time here."

"But I don't want you to take your time. Not right now anyway. Maybe next time."

She was already thinking of next time and his own brain had stalled out on the suddenly complex mechanics of retrieving a condom from the bedside table. Needing to take back some control of the situation, he lowered his head to trail a line of slow kisses along the column of her throat, ending at the tender juncture by her collarbone. Rowan shivered.

She was so unexpectedly soft. Nash loved the contrast of that softness against the tough-as-nails cop he knew her to be. It felt like an erotic secret just between them. He liked the idea of being her secret keeper. He liked just about everything about Rowan Beale.

Just as he inched lower, intent on lavishing some more attention on those glorious breasts of hers, she clamped her legs around his waist and rolled. He could've overpowered her and flipped them back, but he recognized that she was done giving up control. He'd entice her to hand over the reins again later. Right now, the sight of her rising over him, her dark hair tumbled around her shoulders all but stole his breath. Plus, his new position put the nightstand into actual reach. Without taking his eyes off her, Nash reached for the drawer, fumbling around until he came up with a foil packet.

Rowan snatched it from his hand, handily ripping it open and rolling it on. She paused, running her hands over the ridges of his abs and across his pecs. "I'm just gonna say, I appreciate the fact that you haven't stopped PT since you left the Navy."

Nash skimmed his own hands up the toned length of her legs. "Consider me your playground and do with me as you wish." He couldn't imagine anything better than having her use him to satisfy her every carnal desire.

Her lips curved in one of those secretive, female smiles that suggested she was on board with that plan. Scooting up his body, she reached between them to guide him to her entrance. Planting her hands on either side of his head, she began to sink down, taking him in inch by slow, torturous inch. Though every nerve demanded that he touch and take, he held himself perfectly still. She was so tight and hot. He watched her face, searching for any signs of discomfort, but all he saw was a fierce satisfaction as he filled her in a slow rise and fall that finally seated him fully inside her.

She dropped her brow to his as her body stretched and eased around him. "God, you feel amazing. I could stay right here, exactly like this, for a long damn time."

"I might die." It felt like a very real possibility, trapped, unmoving, in the hot prison of her body. Nash couldn't stop the tremble in his body from the strain of holding himself back.

Grinning, she brushed her lips to his. "Can't have that."

So, she took him at his word, using him for her pleasure until they were both slicked with sweat and mindless of anything but the touch and taste of each other. And as she bowed back, lost in him, her body clamping around his, Nash thought himself found and followed her over the edge.

Later, a long time later, he came back to himself. All the tension she'd been carrying since she walked into his life had dissipated. For now, at least. She lay draped over him, a warm blanket of woman. He skimmed his hand along her spine, stroking that soft, soft skin and wishing she could stay. But they both knew she had responsibilities. Responsibilities she'd need to get back to. He knew she'd already made up her mind about that even as she sucked in a breath.

"At the risk of destroying a lovely afterglow, I should be getting back." She rolled away from him, and Nash immediately missed her heat.

He sat up himself, scooping hands through his hair. "I'll drive you next door."

Rowan huffed a laugh as she located her bra. "If you think Robert didn't notice your truck getting back, you don't know him very well. He knows I've been over here."

Nash stiffened. "We could've been watching a movie."

"We could've." The heated look she shot him had Nash wanting to drag her back to bed for some more alternatives to Hollywood entertainment. "But I'm banking that he's not that stupid either."

"I don't wanna think about that." Robert still had firearms in the house.

"I sure as hell don't intend to talk about it. And I don't think he will either. My love life is none of his business, and I have no trouble telling him so, should it come up."

Nash fervently hoped it didn't come up.

In the end, he walked her home, enjoying holding her hand as they strolled up his drive and across the street. She'd tidied her hair and didn't look as thoroughly rumpled as she had in his bed. He already wanted to see her there again.

On the porch, she turned to face him. "I had fun tonight."

"Me too. We should do it again."

A flash of humor crossed her face.

Nash leaned close. "Get your mind out of the gutter."

She was smiling as he kissed her, and he considered that a victory for the night.

"See you tomorrow, Flyboy."

"Tomorrow," he agreed.

CHAPTER 8

*A*t the crack of gunfire, Rowan jolted awake. Heart threatening to beat straight out of her chest, she hit the floor, cracking her knee on the hardwood and automatically covering her head before she was even truly conscious. Awareness of where she was slammed into her. Robert's. She was in the guest room at Robert's.

Nightmare. It was just a nightmare.

On a slow exhale, she dropped her brow to the floor.

Another two shots shattered the stillness of night. Rowan jerked her head up, pulse kicking back to high gear.

Not a nightmare. Someone was shooting at the house.

A thud sounded from down the hall, launching her heart into her throat.

Oh God, oh no, oh shit. Was someone *in* the house?

Rowan kicked free of the covers tangled around her legs and rose into a crouch, retrieving the case with her Sig Sauer from the nightstand drawer. Her fingers fumbled through the combination.

"C'mon. C'mon!"

Snick.

The lock sprang open, and she pulled out the gun, sliding in a fresh magazine. Though she wanted to race, she forced herself to slow down, clear the rooms as she made her way down the hall to Robert's bedroom. Prepared for the worst, she opened the door, immediately ducking to make herself a smaller target.

Robert lay on the floor, gasping for breath, clutching his chest. Rowan swept the room. No intruder. No shattered glass.

She didn't have time to make sense of that as she knelt by her great uncle. No blood. But that was only a minor relief. His pulse thundered every bit as hard as hers, and his face was pale, even in the moonlight streaming through the windows.

"It's gonna be okay, Unk. I'm getting help." *Please don't let me be too late.*

Keeping out of the line of sight of the windows, she grabbed the cordless phone from one of the nightstands and dialed 9-1-1 as she hurried back to Robert.

"9-1-1, what is the nature of your emergency?"

"Multiple shots have been fired outside 1137 Boydell Road, and I need an ambulance for a fifty-five-year-old man having a heart attack."

"Can the shooter get into the house?"

"I..." Damn it. She hadn't checked the doors.

With a quick look at Robert, she bolted to the front of the house, then to the back door in the kitchen. Both locked. "No. As best I can tell, no one has come inside."

"Is the heart attack patient breathing?"

Rowan ran back down the hall and dropped to her knees beside him. "Yes, but it's extremely labored, and his color is terrible. His pulse is strong but very fast. He just had bypass surgery three weeks ago."

Rowan could hear the rapid clacking of a keyboard.

"Is the shooter immediately outside?"

"I don't know."

"Did you just hear the shots, or did you see someone?"

Questions. Endless questions. As a cop she knew they had to be asked, but she just wanted them to send someone... "The sound woke me up, then I heard two more."

"So, you didn't see anyone?"

"No." God, she was every useless witness she'd ever interviewed.

"Do you have any idea who the shooter might be?"

Rowan considered who might have followed her from Houston, but there was no sense getting into that now. "No."

"Which direction did the shots come from?"

"North, I think. From the back side of the house. They sounded close." And yet how was it there was no shattered glass? The sound had been so loud, she'd swear someone was shooting *at* the house.

"Okay, police are on their way. The fire department and ambulance are right behind, but they will not come to the scene until the police clear them."

"Understood." Rowan bit back the need to urge them to hurry. They'd get here as soon as they could.

Please don't be too late.

She wanted to go outside herself, to track down whoever the fuck had done this, but she didn't dare leave Robert. As soon as the dispatcher finished giving her instructions for her great uncle, she disconnected and dialed Nash.

He answered on the first ring. "What's wrong?" Was he one of those guys who sounded wide awake when you woke him in the middle of the night?

Everything. "Robert's having another heart attack."

"I'm coming over."

"No! I don't know where the shooter is." What if he'd withdrawn to the woods and was just waiting to pick off anyone to come out of or up to the house?

"Shooter? What shooter?" Nash's voice went sharp, and she could hear him shifting into tactical mode.

"Someone was shooting at the house. It's what woke me up."

The long beat of silence had her gut clenching even tighter.

"Rowan, I've been awake since you left. I didn't hear a thing."

She couldn't let the implications of that sink in. Not yet. She had to focus on the thing she knew with certainty was real. Robert needed medical attention. "The police and medical are on their way. I have to go."

Without another word, she hung up the phone.

Bending low over her uncle, she gripped his hand hard. "Don't you dare die on me."

But Robert didn't squeeze her hand back. He'd slipped into unconsciousness.

As the phone clicked to silence, Nash swore. Pausing only to arm himself and throw on some shoes and his Kevlar vest, he slipped out of his own house and ran toward Robert's. If there was a shooter, he'd be unlikely to expect someone approaching on foot. An actual shooter was probably already gone by now. Unless the mission was to kill rather than harass.

Was there really a shooter? Was there a mission?

If someone had used a suppressor, the sound wouldn't have carried all the way to his house. But Rowan had said the sound of shooting woke her. Maybe she meant the sound of bullets striking the house or breaking a window. Until confronted with evidence that said otherwise, he had to assume he was stepping into a dangerous situation.

Toward the end of his driveway, he moved into the woods, intending to approach from the left flank. A shooter with any brains would be firing from the cover of trees. Slowing his pace, Nash scanned the area. Lights were still off in the house. Rowan would be keeping low, making sure not to highlight them both as prospective targets to anyone looking inside. He wished he'd grabbed a flashlight, though that would've just as easily made him a target. How far out was backup?

As his eyes adjusted to the darkness, he circled the perimeter of the house. He didn't see any movement. He didn't find signs of anything by the time two more Wishful PD officers pulled up a few minutes later, followed by Chief Greer. Nash announced himself and gave a quick report.

"Have you seen Robert?" Ethan asked.

"Not yet."

"Fire and medical are staging off-site, waiting for our go ahead. Let's make another sweep to ensure the scene is secure. Caller believes the shots were fired from the north side of the house."

The second, more thorough sweep turned up nothing. The only footprints they found were Nash's. Ethan radioed the okay to the medical personnel. "Let's go talk to Rowan."

She answered the door armed. Her face was pale, with lines carved around her unsmiling mouth and eyes hard as marble. But her hands didn't shake as she looked from Ethan to Nash.

"Everything's clear," Ethan told her.

As he spoke, the ambulance pulled into the drive, lights flashing.

Looking beyond him to help, she smoothly lowered the gun and opened the door. Nash didn't miss that she avoided his gaze as they came inside.

"Robert?"

One sharp, short glance. "Unconscious."

The paramedics rushed into the house. Rowan led them down the hall to Robert's room, then stepped back as they did their thing.

"Tell me what happened," Ethan ordered.

With one last look into Robert's room, she edged down the hall and into her own room. Nash and Ethan followed. She switched on a lamp. The covers were dragged half off the bed and the nightstand drawer hung open. A lockbox lay abandoned on the floor. Rowan strode over and picked it up.

"I got back late. Around eleven. My great uncle had already gone to bed. I went to sleep myself, and I woke up hearing gunshots."

"Do you know what time that was?"

"One seventeen. I saw the clock. I thought at first it was a nightmare, then I heard two more shots, followed by a thud from the other room. Robert falling out of bed, I assume. I grabbed my gun and went to check on him." As she spoke, she smoothly ejected the bullet in the chamber of the Sig and released the magazine, placing it all neatly back in the case. "There was no sign of anyone inside, and he was on the floor, clearly in distress. I called 9-1-1." Her recitation was flat, almost robotic.

Nash studied her, wondering if she was in shock or if she was hanging on to cop mode to maintain some kind of control.

"Were there any further shots after you called 9-1-1?"

"No."

Ethan turned to Nash. "You were just across the street. Did you hear anything?"

What else could he say but the truth? "No."

Rowan did look at him then, skewering him with her eyes. He wanted to protest that answering honestly wasn't a betrayal, but she wasn't in any mood to see it that way.

Wheels echoed in the hall as the emergency medical staff rushed the gurney toward the front door.

"I'm going with them." Rowan fell into step behind them.

"I'll meet you at the hospital," Nash told her.

She didn't even look back. "Don't bother."

He stood, rooted in place as she climbed into the ambulance.

She's upset, he reasoned. She'd calm down once she knew Robert was in the clear. Because he didn't want to dwell overmuch on what it would do to her if he wasn't in the clear and because he knew she needed answers, Nash threw himself into work, coordinating with his fellow officers to process the scene.

In the end they found no shell casings, no bullet holes, no slugs, no evidence of a sniper's nest. Not even any footprints other than their own. He and Ethan even headed back to his house to check the footage from the cameras.

Nothing but the doe that habitually wandered through the yard. It spooked a few minutes before 1:17.

As Nash stopped the video, Ethan sat back. "We've got no evidence of a shooter."

"That deer spooked at something"

"You and I both know that could've been a coyote or any number of other critters. There's no hard evidence."

"No." And damn, he'd actually wanted something—anything so that there was another answer besides the one he was left with.

"I talked to her captain," Ethan continued. "He firmly believes she's suffering from PTSD in the wake of her partner's death."

"She told you they'd say that."

Ethan crossed his arms. "You've spent time with her. What do you think?"

Nash scrubbed a hand over his hair. What *did* he think? "She's been through a helluva lot the last few months. I think it all took a bigger toll on her than she's willing to admit." He thought of her nightmares. She was still playing the events of that night over in her head. But talking about that did feel like a betrayal. "I don't know if she has PTSD. But I know she's worried to death about Robert's health. His condition is real enough. You saw him."

"Yeah." Ethan blew out a breath. "Whatever this is, I don't like it. Neither option is good. I've either got some trigger-happy son of a bitch terrorizing some of my citizens or a woman with some prospectively dangerous delusions who could become unstable."

"I don't think she's unstable." Nash did feel confident in saying that.

"Well, time will tell. We'll go over the area again in the morning, when we've got daylight. Maybe we missed something. Meanwhile, I figure you're ready to head to the hospital."

"She told me not to come." And he was man enough to admit that had stung. They'd been friends, and after earlier tonight, he'd thought they were on their way to maybe being more. But at the first sign of trouble, she was throwing up blinking neon signs shouting *Back the hell off.*

Ethan arched a brow. "You gonna let that stop you?"

Nash paused. "Well, I reckon she will need a ride since she went in the ambulance with him."

"That's the spirit. See you tomorrow."

CHAPTER 9

*R*owan held it together on the ride to the hospital. She clung to her control by fingernails as they rushed him inside, behind the automatically locking doors leading to the operating rooms. Arms wrapped around herself, she'd stood there staring after them until a nurse had kindly pointed her to a chair in the waiting area. She hadn't called her parents or grandfather. There was no point until she had something concrete to tell them. When another nurse came to tell her that he'd regained consciousness, she'd cried with relief. She'd been certain he wouldn't wake up again, and she'd been so very afraid.

The nurse had escorted her behind the doors and into a curtained bay to wait, while the doctors ran some kind of tests. It was then she lost her grip on the panic and began to rock, covering her mouth with one hand to hold in the sounds that wanted to pour out. Rowan didn't know if they were tears or screams, and she was terrified that if she let them out, even an inch, she wouldn't be able to stop.

She'd heard gunshots. She knew she had. Hadn't she? But Nash's house was close enough that he'd have heard, especially if he was awake, as he'd said. The sounds she'd heard weren't suppressed shots.

So maybe she was crazy. Maybe her nightmares were bleeding into her waking hours. That was a thing. One of the possible symptoms of PTSD, according to Dr. Powers. But she hadn't been having the nightmare. It was that external sound that had woken her up. Wasn't it?

Rowan didn't know. Not for sure. And that not knowing was freaking her the hell out. At least the crazy had meant she'd been awake when Robert fell. She didn't know if she'd have heard that, and he hadn't been in any shape to call out for help.

"Ms. Beale?"

She looked up to find a blonde man in surgical scrubs and a lab coat, with a clipboard in hand. Digging deep, she found some scraps of control and lowered her hand. "Yes?"

"I'm Dr. Phillips."

"How's my uncle?"

She must have been doing okay on appearances because Dr. Phillips came in to sit on the rolling stool in the corner, without looking alarmed at her behavior. "He's stable."

"Was it another heart attack?" Rowan braced herself for the answer, wishing Nash were here, then feeling foolish. He thought she was crazy. She didn't need him.

"Actually, no."

She didn't know whether to be relieved or more concerned. "Then what was it? Some kind of complication from his bypass surgery?"

"We believe it was a panic attack."

Rowan blinked. Surely, she hadn't heard him right. "A panic attack? Why would he be having a panic attack?"

"We don't know. He was still a little out of it while we were questioning him, and he's resting now. But you can certainly ask him when he wakes up. It's not actually uncommon among cardiac patients. There's considerable fear about having another, and that can sometimes lead to something that feels like a self-fulfilling prophecy. We want to keep him at least overnight for observation, as there are some levels we want to check, and just as a general precaution to make sure there are no complications from his fall."

"Okay." That made her feel better. In her current state, she wasn't sure she could rest at all, and she didn't trust herself to catch a problem if one arose.

"We've admitted him and transferred him to a room on the second floor. There's some more paperwork for you to fill out."

Of course, there was. Rowan just nodded. "I'm staying here tonight." She wouldn't have left him and either way, she'd told Nash not to come, so she had no ride.

"I'll see that they bring another blanket and pillow. The chair in the room folds out. I can't call it a bed, but it's horizontal at least."

"I'm sure it'll be fine. Thank you, Dr. Phillips."

Rowan filled out the paperwork. By the time she'd finished that, the adrenaline she'd been running on for the past couple of hours had waned, leaving her punchy and exhausted. Another nurse led her to her great uncle's room, where a blanket and pillow were folded on the vinyl chair.

Robert lay sleeping in a hospital bed. Assorted machines were lined up like sentinels, beeping out the comforting rhythm of a steady heartbeat. He snored faintly. For a long time, Rowan just stood there, watching him, silently giving thanks that he was okay. She'd let the rest of the family know in the morning. No reason to worry them with a phone call in the middle of the night.

With minimal fuss, she flattened the chair and tried to make herself comfortable with the wafer-thin pillow and rough blanket. How did anyone sleep in hospitals? Was it all a matter of being too drugged to care that this stuff didn't offer even a modicum of legitimate comfort?

They'd tried to do that for the couple of days she'd been hospitalized after her rescue, but she hadn't gone for it. She didn't want anything dulling her mind. But after tonight, faced with the very real prospect that she truly did have the problems they suspected, that she really wasn't fit for duty, she could see the appeal.

Not that she could or would ask for anything.

Her mind drifted to Nash. She'd shut him out. After everything they'd shared, it had sliced her to the bone to see him look at her as if she really were crazy, with that faint expression of concerned sympathy. He was a good man. She knew that. She'd called, and he'd immediately come. She'd seen him checking the scene before the rest of the police had arrived. But she couldn't bear to look at him and know he thought she was damaged goods. Because if he thought that, she didn't have a choice but to believe it herself.

THE HOSPITAL WAS QUIET, nowhere near visiting hours by the time Nash went in search of Rowan. He got the hairy eyeball from the nurse he asked about Robert, until he explained he was here to pick up the woman who'd ridden with him in the ambulance. Then she relented and gave him the room number. He took the stairs, remembering the other hospital stairwell he'd climbed with her in Lawley and that moment she'd let him comfort her. He wondered if she'd let him do that again or if she'd snap back at him still. She needed someone's support in all of this.

Robert's room was predictably dark and quiet, lit by the faint glow of light from the bathroom and the LED displays on the assorted machines the older man was hooked up to. Their beeping and readouts seemed calm and steady. That was good, right?

Rowan was curled up on one of those God-awful convertible chairs in the corner. Her soft inhalations were a quiet counterpoint to the louder snores of her great uncle. She didn't look relaxed, exactly—who would on that questionable slab of furniture?—but she didn't look distressed either. Maybe he ought to leave her be and wait until morning. It wasn't that far off.

He could probably find a corner somewhere to catch a few z's. It wasn't as if he hadn't slept under worse conditions in the Navy. He'd grab two or three hours and greet her with coffee from the cafeteria when it opened.

"Nash."

Her eyes were open, watching him back.

"Hi," he whispered.

She sat up, the hospital blanket pooling around her waist. "I told you not to come."

She'd had a lousy few hours, so he chose not to be offended by that. Ever the optimist. "Tough shit. I didn't listen."

That seemed to flummox her.

"How is he?"

Rowan looked at Robert for a long moment before shoving to her feet and crossing over to where Nash stood just inside the door. Her arms crossed over her belly instead of her chest in a gesture of self-protection rather than belligerence. "He's okay. It wasn't another heart attack. They wanted to keep him overnight for observation."

Nash wanted to pull her into his arms, but she'd clearly thrown up walls since she'd left his bed. Beyond the fact that she was pissed at him, he hated that her chance at relaxation had lasted so little time. The strain of the past few hours had etched itself on her face, much as he'd seen it when she first arrived.

"Do they know what it actually was?"

"A panic attack, apparently. The doctor said it isn't uncommon for heart attack patients." She pulled her gaze off Robert and finally looked at him. "What about the investigation?"

Nash didn't want to talk about this. He didn't want to quash whatever her final hope was that someone else was behind all this. But she deserved the truth. "We found no evidence of a shooter. No bullet holes. No shell casings. There was nothing on the cameras."

Her mouth tightened. "You think it's all in my head."

"I didn't say that." But it was what he was thinking, and they both knew it.

"You didn't have to." She turned away, but not before he'd seen the anguish on her face.

Nash couldn't stand it. He reached out to curve his hands around her shoulders, turning her back to face him. "Rowan...you've been through a lot. It could've been a nightmare. There's no shame in that."

She remained stiff, her hands curling to fists. "It wasn't a goddamned nightmare. I know the difference. I've relived that day over and over. I know what I heard then. It wasn't what I heard tonight. I heard gunshots, at least three in relative succession. I was awake, Nash. So, either there was a shooter or..." She sucked in a breath. "Or I'm crazy."

He cupped her cheek, wanting to do anything to make her feel better. "Trauma doesn't make you crazy."

"It makes me unfit for duty." Those pain-filled eyes closed, and tears slid from the corners, effectively shredding his guts.

Nash pulled her into his arms, wrapping her tight. After a moment's hesitation, she burrowed in, pressing her face to his chest. He could feel her shaking and didn't know if it was from the effort of trying not to cry or from trying to do it without making a sound. He knew what this meant to her. Being a cop was everything. If she couldn't go back to doing that, what would she do? Christ, how could he fix this for her?

A rumble of sound came from the bed. "Not a nightmare. Not crazy. Outside my room."

They broke apart and hurried to the bed, flanking Robert on either side.

Rowan took his hand. "What?"

He swallowed. "Heard gunshots outside my room."

She shot a startled glance up at Nash, before looking back at her great uncle. "You heard them, too?" There was no hiding the urgency in her tone.

"Scared the shit out of me. Fell out of bed right onto the damned floor." He scowled.

"You heard them," Rowan repeated. Then again, in a softer voice. "You heard them." When she met Nash's gaze again, her expression held a fragile hope.

He reached out to take her free hand, squeezing tight. "You're not crazy."

"Somebody get me some water and then tell me what the hell is going on," Robert demanded.

CHAPTER 10

"*Y*ou haven't been honest with me."

Rowan flinched, though her great uncle's words were more statement of fact than accusation. "No."

"Why?"

"Because you'd have worried, and you already had enough stress. See also, two heart attacks in the past four months." She gestured toward his chest.

"Tell me now."

She dropped her gaze and fiddled with the tab on the can of Coke Nash had brought back from the vending machine. "There was more to that bad call where Reyes died than I let on." She stopped, wondering where to start. Wondering *how* to start. She'd spent so much of the past few months keeping everything locked down tight, telling no one because she didn't know whom she could trust.

Nash's warm hand settled on her shoulder and squeezed. She wanted to lean into him, lean *on* him. But she saw Robert take in the touch, his expression inscrutable. Her involvement with Nash was something else she didn't want to talk about, but she laid her hand over his and squeezed once in thanks for the support.

"Before the raid where I was rescued, I heard something. A guy high up in our Narcotics Division arguing with the gang leader, wanting to know why the hell I wasn't dead yet. That my being there endangered the entire operation. I went under again before I got any more, and then the next thing I knew, the whole place was swarming with law enforcement."

"How did you know it was him?" Robert asked. "Do you know him?"

"Not super well. He conducted one of my trainings in my early days on the force. But he has a very distinctive voice. I didn't imagine it. So, I reported what I'd heard, and Internal Affairs opened an investigation. But nothing came of it. He'd been undercover with the gang for months and nothing I overheard indicated they knew he was a cop. The whole thing was explained away as him protecting his cover. Which was also why he wasn't part of the raid himself."

"You didn't mention that part when you told us about this before," Nash broke in.

Rowan glanced at him. "I didn't mention a lot of things."

"Us?" Robert prompted.

"Nash and Chief Greer. I'll circle back to that."

"Okay. You don't buy that explanation about the guy." Robert didn't sound judgmental about it.

"No. I don't have any solid evidence to back up my version of things. It's just my word, my gut feeling that he's dirty. David didn't trust him, but he never said why. And now he's dead. Maybe it's a coincidence. Maybe not. But I believe, down to my bones, that Trent Voss is a dirty cop." That belief hadn't wavered at any point.

"When I woke up earlier, you said something about feeling crazy. What was that about?"

"I didn't make any friends with my accusations. I've been ostracized in the department and subject to a string of harassment, the evidence of which conveniently disappeared every time I tried to report it. Between that and my trying to turn Voss in, my credibility is shot. I haven't been allowed back in the field since it happened, and at this rate, I don't know if I ever will be. The department shrink refuses to sign off on the psych eval and recommended an extended leave of absence. That happened to coincide with your latest heart attack, so I didn't fight about it. I figured I'd take care of you and decompress. And when nothing happened here, she'd be forced to admit it wasn't all in my head. Except the harassment didn't stop when I got here."

Rowan explained about the graffiti on his truck, the spray paint on her hoodie, and the cameras she and Nash had set up. She even told him about her sleepwalking. "It's been quiet since then. Until tonight. I know what I heard, but there is literally no evidence to support it."

"Except that I heard it, too."

"Except that," she agreed. And thank God for it. She'd been losing what felt like an ever more tenuous grip on her sanity.

Nash spoke up. "It's a smart tactic. Back in Houston, it was easier to get to her, easier for her to maintain someone else was behind everything. But with a change in location, that becomes harder to justify. What better way to convince her she's crazy than to follow her here and continue to gaslight her?"

"But what I don't understand is, if Voss or

someone connected to him did this, how did he know to follow me here? I didn't take a traceable commercial flight. You came to get me."

"You didn't tell anyone where you were going? No friends? Whoever you turned in your leave to?"

Rowan shook her head. "No. I just took the leave. I didn't tell anybody where I was going...except—well I didn't tell her, but I was in Dr. Powers' office when Mom called about the heart attack."

"That's the department shrink?" Robert asked.

"Yeah."

"How much about all this does she know?"

Rowan stared at her great uncle, realization dawning. "Almost all of it. I didn't talk about the emotional shit because that's what I figured was keeping me on the desk. But the harassment, the ostracism...she knows about all of that. But surely..."

"Who better to undermine your credibility?" Robert suggested.

That thought made her even more uncomfortable about the therapist than she already had been. "I don't know if I buy that. What motive would she have?"

Robert shrugged. "Don't know. Maybe she's involved with Voss. Might be romantic, might be friends, might just be in on whatever the hell Voss is up to. Fact is, if one cop in the department is dirty, others might be, too. And Houston is a *big* department. Either way, somebody clearly followed you to Wishful, and we need to decide what to do about it."

"Yeah, but what?"

Nash had been largely silent for most of the explanation. At this, he straightened. "I've got an idea."

NASH SLID BACK into the driver's seat. "How long do you think it'll take Robert to figure out that we convinced the doctor to keep him at the hospital under supervision?"

Rowan shut the door and crossed another name off their list. "Hopefully long enough for us to get through Phase 1 of your plan."

They'd spent the morning quietly checking everywhere somebody might legally stay to see if someone with a Texas driver's license had registered in the past three weeks. Nash didn't know if they'd get a hit or not. If their perp or perps thought their gaslighting campaign was successful, they might not expect Rowan to follow up on this kind of a lead. They might have gotten sloppy. Or he and Rowan were running around on a wild goose chase. Either way, it made her feel like she was doing something active instead of waiting for the next thing to happen.

"He's gonna be pissed," Nash observed. "He doesn't want a babysitter."

"I can handle him pissed. I've been handling his grumpy ass for weeks. Whether he likes it or not, he's not up to full strength. So far, they haven't targeted him, but I'm not willing to risk it."

"Fair enough." Cranking the truck, Nash pulled out of the parking lot of the Mockingbird Motel. "With the Babylon and the motel crossed off, all we've got left around Wishful is the campground and RV park up near Hope Springs. If we don't get a hit there, we may need to cast a wider net."

The drive to the campground took a while, as they had to circle around the massive lake to the opposite side. Rowan stayed quiet. Nash couldn't get a read on whether she was pensive, worried, or just plain tired. Neither of them had gotten much sleep last night.

"I'm sorry." She didn't look at him as she spoke.

"For what?"

"For how I acted. For shutting you out. You've been nothing but kind and supportive through everything, and I..." She trailed off on a frustrated sigh.

"You reacted. That's human. Somebody's working really damned hard to make you doubt yourself, and I played right into that."

"Still, I've had few enough allies in this, and I shouldn't have snapped. So, I'm sorry." She finally glanced his way. "For what it's worth, I'm really glad I'm not in this alone anymore."

Nash reached out to tangle his fingers with hers. "Me, too."

"I want it over. I want my life back. And I think—maybe—when I get to that point, I want to leave Houston."

He had to force himself to keep his eyes on the road, his voice nonchalant. "Yeah?"

"Even if I'm proved right, I'll never go back to being a part of that department. There are people there who will never trust me again. I don't want to stay in an environment like that. I don't think I can."

She wanted to leave Houston. It was way the hell too soon to push her for whether that meant she wanted to come here. There was too much up in the air, too much left to be resolved. And they were...well, he didn't know exactly what they were yet.

"Does it hurt?"

That startled him enough to look at her. The corners of her mouth were quirked in the barest of smiles.

"Does what hurt?"

"Where you were biting your tongue. I know you're thinking about that open position at Wishful PD. Robert mentioned it to me, too."

"I'm not here to pressure you about anything."

"No, you wouldn't. That's not your way, is it?"

"Not generally."

She looked away again. "I wasn't looking for you. But here you are. Here *this* is." Her fingers squeezed around his. "So yeah, I'm factoring that into the equation when I think about my next move."

His lips curved. "Can't ask for more than that." Not yet, anyway.

The "office" of the campground was an RV that apparently stayed in place year-round. Being on this side of the lake, it was technically out of his jurisdiction, but he hoped the manager would be cooperative. Nash knocked on the door.

A balding man in an ancient cardigan answered, a pair of glasses sliding down his nose. "Help you?"

"Hope so, sir. I'm Officer Brewer, Wishful Police Department. This is Officer Beale. We're investigating a shooting—"

"A shooting! Where? Did somebody die?"

Rowan picked up the thread. "We're not at liberty to say, sir. But we have reason to believe that the perpetrator may have been staying somewhere in or around Wishful over the past three weeks. We're checking anywhere that might have had vacancies during that time to see if someone registered with a Texas driver's license or car tag."

"Well now, we don't have a lot of traffic this time of year. Can't say as I remember where the few we've had were from. People come from all over, you know."

"Yes, sir. Do you maintain any records you could check?" Nash prompted.

"I'll get the book." The guy disappeared inside, returning a minute later with a binder. He was frowning. "That's odd. The most recent page is missing."

Nash and Rowan exchanged a look. Rowan held out her hand. "If I may, sir?"

The guy passed the binder over.

"Anybody got a pencil?"

Nash retrieved one from the truck. As Rowan lightly rubbed the lead over the blank page, their host looked at Nash with a frown. "Say, why aren't you in a patrol car?"

"We're down one in the fleet. Couple months back, our rookie swerved to miss a cow in the road and ran it up a tree. I've got a light on the dash in the meantime." He pointed, and that seemed to satisfy the guy. He was doubly glad they'd stopped back by his place for him to change into his uniform.

"Bingo," Rowan announced. "One Philip McCoskey with a Texas tag. Looks like he's out of Lubbock. Stayed here a little over two weeks ago." She tipped the binder to show the indentions from the missing page. "God bless old school record keeping. Can I keep this page?"

"I don't see why not."

As she tore out the page with the information, Nash picked up the questioning. "Do you remember Mr. McCoskey?"

"He was a quiet guy. Kept to himself."

"Can you describe him at all?"

The middle-aged man shoved his glasses up his nose. "Older guy. Short hair. Dark, with a smattering of gray. Maybe ex-military or something."

"What makes you say that?" Rowan asked.

"He was in really good shape, and he just had that way of moving. Like he could handle himself."

"Did you notice anything odd about his accent?"

"His accent? No, not especially. He was southern, but not from around here."

"Did he happen to say what he was doing in the area?" Nash asked.

"He said he was here to do some hunting. Paid cash for a campsite for two nights and slept in his truck. One of those deals with a camper top."

"Do you remember what color?"

"Black. Or maybe dark blue."

"Can you think of anything else that might help us find this guy?" Nash urged.

"No. I'm sorry, I wasn't paying that close attention. There was a big group of retirees up partying late that week. All my focus was on them."

"That's all right," Rowan assured him. "If you think of anything else, you can call us at this number." She handed over a card.

"Do I need to be worried?"

"There's no reason to think he'll come back here. But if he does, let us know, will you?" she said.

"I sure will."

"Thank you for your help, Mr...." Nash offered his hand.

"Underwood. Silas Underwood."

"Mr. Underwood. You have a good day, now."

Back in the truck, Rowan studied the page. "What are the chances that somebody from Texas happens to show up at that campground, at that time? It matches up with the vandalism to Robert's truck."

"Seems pretty slim to me. What about Underwood's description? You think this could be our guy?"

"It was pretty vague, but it could be him. I think this name is an alias and the tag will probably come back stolen."

"One way to find out." Nash whipped out his phone and dialed the station.

CHAPTER 11

"Are you sure about this?"

Rowan took in Nash's worried face. "As sure as I am about anything. Your dispatcher confirmed the stolen plates, and there's no evidence that McCoskey's a real guy. If he's still in the area, we want to push him to act."

"Maybe we should run this plan by Robert first."

"I'll tell him about it when I go pick him up." Without waiting for further comment, she dialed the number she never imagined ever calling.

"Hello, this is Dr. Powers."

At the sound of the psychologist's voice, a hot flash of anger ripped through Rowan. Had this woman betrayed her confidence? Violated her professional ethics? This whole plan hinged on the answers to those questions being yes.

"Hello?"

"Dr. Powers, this is Rowan Beale. I—" She didn't have to feign reluctance. Telling this woman anything had always been a challenge. "I didn't know who else to call."

"Rowan, I'm so pleased to hear from you. How is your...I wasn't clear on who had a medical issue in your family when you left."

"He's stable." She wasn't about to drop any more information about Robert into this conversation. "That's not why I called."

"Oh?" The faint tone of interest and surprise did nothing to cover the sharpening of the woman's attention.

"I...I've been having these flashes. About my time in captivity. I remembered more about what happened."

"You did? What did you remember?"

"I know everybody thinks I'm crazy. That my accusations against Voss are unfounded, but this...It's so much worse than I originally thought." Rowan let her voice shake. Let the woman believe she was afraid.

"I'm so glad you called me with this. That you're reaching out on your own—that's progress. Good progress." She had that good-dog sort of tone again that set Rowan's teeth on edge. "Why don't you take me through what-ever it is you think you remember before you choose to act on it."

"I don't just think I remember!"

The therapist remained patient in the face of Rowan's predictable snap. "You've been through a trauma. We've discussed this. The mind can play tricks on you. Something that you believe is a memory could be utterly false, just a way for your brain to process the things that happened to you."

Rowan's irritation was genuine. "I'm not crazy. I know how to prove everything."

"As before, Rowan, these are very serious accusations. I think you need to tell me every-thing so we can decide the best way to handle this."

"There's no 'we,' Dr. Powers. You don't have a say in this."

"I know you don't want me to, but Rowan, you've had enough problems in the department from what's already happened. If you go off half-cocked, without seriously thinking this through, even I won't be able to talk them into keeping you on."

Right. Like she'd expended so much effort on actually helping Rowan already. But Rowan understood the warning, the implied threat that was meant to keep her under control. It was nice to get confirmation that her decision to leave Houston was the right one.

"This was a mistake. I shouldn't have called."

"Ro—"

But Rowan hung up before she could con-tinue. "God, I hate that woman. But whatever, now we see if they take the bait. And if, as we suspect, there is a 'they' to begin with. If she's in league with Voss, the news that I can prove his involvement should be enough to force his hand. Assuming he's still here."

Nash's expression was grim. "I don't like using you as bait."

"It'll be fine. I'm a good cop."

He cupped her face between his palms. "You could be the best cop on the planet, and I still wouldn't like this."

Her stomach did a slow roll at the look in his eyes. Because he needed reassurance and because she didn't know what to do with how that look made her feel, she curled her hands into his uniform shirt and offered a cocky grin. "I won't take that personally."

"I sure as hell hope you will."

Her grin faded. "Nash..."

He kissed her, and she could taste his barely leashed frustration and worry. But his hold remained gentle. That contrast was a sign of the control she didn't give him nearly enough credit for. She loved that he understood she didn't want him to step in and take over. Loved, too, that he'd stay back and let her do what she needed to do. She suspected she could learn to love a helluva lot about Nash Brewer if only she gave them a real chance.

He broke the kiss and pressed his brow to hers. "I said I wouldn't push, and I meant it. But I give a damn about what happens to you. I don't want you hurt, and I don't like that you won't have me watching your six the rest of the day. If there was anybody who could cover my shift, I'd do it."

"I'll be fine. I'm just going to spring Robert from the hospital and come back here to the house. We can barricade ourselves in. Absolutely nothing has been done here until after dark. There's no reason to believe that he'd be so rash as to violate that now. That'd be stupid, and Voss is anything but stupid."

Nash checked his watch and frowned. "I

have to get going. Call me when you get home, okay? Just to let me know you made it."

"Okay." She rose to her toes and brushed her lips over his one last time. "Go on. You'll be late."

"See you tonight."

It felt odd seeing him off to work. Odd, but kind of nice. What would it be like if she were hired on here? That could be either awesome or awful. With him as a reserve officer, they probably wouldn't actually work together all that often. But it would be nice to have that commonality.

No need to get ahead of yourself, Beale. There's nothing that says Ethan Greer will hire you on in the first place. Right now, he probably thinks you're just as nuts as everybody in Houston does.

But God willing, this plan would work, and she'd flush Voss or whoever was harassing her out of hiding and push him into making a mistake. And when he did, she'd be ready.

Feeling confident and hopeful for the first

time in months, she grabbed Robert's truck keys and went to liberate him from the hospital.

The parking lot was full. It seemed like hospital parking lots always were. She didn't want Robert walking that far, but once they got through the discharge process, she'd come get the truck and pull it around to the main doors. Decided, she took one of the few empty spaces at the far end of the lot. Pocketing the keys, she trudged toward the hospital, pulling out her phone as she wove through the rows of cars. She'd just send Nash a text to let him know she was here.

Maybe, once Robert was settled and the house sufficiently barricaded, she could carve out time for a nap. Last night's lack of sleep was really beginning to catch up with her. She might even be able to talk Robert into giving her a turn in The Chair—

Lightning shot through her body, electrifying nerves into pure agony. Her muscles convulsed, and she began to fall. But instead of hitting the ground, she was pulled against a solid chest.

"They should have done away with you like I told them," someone growled. "But as usual, if I want something done right, I have to do it myself."

She'd made a mistake. As her captor shoved her into the floorboard of a truck, Rowan heard her great uncle's voice in her head. *Never make assumptions as a cop. You'll miss something.*

She'd assumed Voss would stay smart and wait until the cover of night to act.

She'd assumed wrong.

SHE SHOULD HAVE CALLED by now.

Nash checked his watch again as he wrapped a call about package theft. Surely discharge shouldn't take more than two hours. It wasn't like when Robert had been released after bypass surgery. This should have been simple. Sign a few releases and go.

Before he pulled away from the curb, he called her. No answer. It might mean nothing. There was probably a logical explanation. But he couldn't shake the bad feeling that had lodged in his gut, so he headed for the hospital. If she wasn't there, he'd check back at the house.

The parking lot was packed. He drove up and down the aisles, scanning vehicles. When he saw Robert's truck on the last row, the knot in his belly unclenched. She was still here. But why? This morning, they'd convinced the doctor to manufacture some excuse to keep Robert here. Had something else happened?

Finding a space himself, Nash hurried into the building and up to the second floor. Robert turned from the window of his room, fingers drumming against one leg, lips set in a thin line. "It's about damned time. I'm ready to get the hell out of here."

"What's taking so long?"

"Hell if I know. I was ready to go this morning."

"Where's Rowan?"

Robert paused in his pacing. "She's not with you?"

"No. Not for a couple of hours. I had to start my shift. She was leaving to pick you up right after I left for work. Your truck's down in the parking lot."

"Then she's bound to be around here somewhere. Probably harassing my doctor."

That knot in his gut was back. "I'm gonna go see if I can find her."

The truck was here. She had to be here. Right?

The nurse's station was hopping. Given the state of the parking lot, evidently the entire facility was full up. Nash bit back his impatience, waiting until one of the nurses looked his way rather than inserting himself into the conversation and pissing them off.

At last, a plump young woman with a mass of reddish curls pulled into a tail and a spray of freckles across her cheeks took notice. "Can we help you?"

He didn't recognize the woman from this morning. There must've been a shift change. "I'm looking for Rowan Beale. She's the great niece of Robert Curry, down in 217."

"I'm sorry, I don't know her. And I believe Mr. Curry is ready for discharge."

"I know. She was supposed to have been here to do that two hours ago. Her vehicle is in the parking lot downstairs, but Robert hasn't seen her." Nash took a step closer, squaring his shoulders and turning on the authoritative cop. "Have any of the rest of you seen her since first thing this morning?" He gave them a quick description of Rowan.

They all stopped talking and looked at one another. After a few moments' hesitation, they shook their heads.

"No, I don't think so."

"Can you page Dr. Phillips?" Maybe she was talking to the doctor.

"I'm afraid he's in surgery. But we can page Ms. Beale."

"Do that." If she were anywhere in this hospital, she'd be able to hear the announcement and come up here.

But when ten minutes passed and Rowan didn't appear, Nash accepted that something was very, very wrong.

"Mr. Curry, you can't be out of your room right now!"

Nash turned to find Robert striding down the hall. He was looking better, but he was still only a shadow of his normal, forceful self.

"You and I both know they've got no reason to keep me. Officer Brewer is my ride. You just go ahead and get that discharge paperwork."

Okay, maybe more than a shadow. The nurse leapt into motion, and Robert turned to Nash. "You start talking. What did you and Rowan find this morning?"

Nash filled him in on the results of their canvassing efforts. By the time he'd made it through Rowan's plan to use herself as bait, Robert had signed whatever needed signing and dropped into the wheelchair they insisted he use to get to the front door.

"I'll wheel him," Nash told the nurse.

She lifted her hands, and he took hold of the wheelchair's handles, steering them both into the elevator.

"Damned fool girl. She should've waited."

"You think Voss has her." It wasn't a question.

"Don't you?"

"Yeah. Yeah, I do."

"Get the car."

"What exactly are you planning to do? You can't run, can't shoot, can't drive. No offense, Robert, but you're a liability in a fight right now."

"I've still got a perfectly good pair of eyes and a brain. Get the car."

There was no point in arguing. Leaving him just inside the automatic doors, Nash strode through the parking lot. On impulse, he wove his way back toward Robert's truck. He wasn't sure what he was looking for, but he didn't find it. Slapping a hand on the tailgate of the truck, he swore and turned to make his way back to his own truck.

Something glinted in the bright afternoon sun. Nash stepped toward it, angling his head to get a better look. There, beneath the rear tire of a minivan, lay a phone. Crouching, he picked it up and swiped open the screen.

His blood turned to ice.

The screen indicated several missed calls. All from him. This was Rowan's phone.

If they'd needed any further proof that she hadn't left this parking lot of her own volition, this was it.

Bolting for his truck, he cranked it and peeled out of the parking lot, earning a few disapproving and irritated glances from other hospital patrons as he squealed to a stop at the front doors. Robert was already waiting.

He climbed in the front, wincing only a little as he tugged the door closed. "What did you find?"

"Her phone. The son of a bitch has her."

Robert cursed.

"Where would he take her?" Nash demanded.

The former Chief of Police considered. "Drive back to my house."

"You think he'd take her there?"

"I don't know. He's already proved he can get inside, and if he's convinced no one else will be coming around, he might."

Nash threw the truck into drive. "And if they aren't there?"

"Then I can at least get some proper shoes and my gun."

Nash could've reiterated that the recoil from a pistol would be far greater than the five-to-seven-pound weight limit he was still under, but he had a feeling it would've been like arguing with a brick wall. So, he held his silence and drove. On the way, Robert took to the radio himself, passing the details on to Inez Barlow, the dispatcher who'd worked with the department almost as long as he had, and asking her to pass it on to the other officers, as well as sending out a BOLO to the surrounding counties.

"What kind of vehicle did you say he was in?" Robert asked.

"Two weeks ago, it was a dark blue or black truck with a camper top. Same plates I had her run this morning. But I don't know if he's in the same thing this trip."

Robert relayed the message to Inez.

"Just a second. I'm getting another call."

The silence grew taut as they waited. When the radio crackled again, Nash almost jolted.

"Chief, I don't know if this is coincidence or not, but I just had somebody call in a complaint about a reckless driver about eight miles out on County Road 473. A black truck with a camper top. Was speeding and nearly hit the guy on his bike."

Nash hit the brakes and made a quick U-turn, flipping on his dash lights and turning on the siren as he headed toward that side of town.

"We're en route, Inez. Send whoever is on duty as backup."

"Yes, Chief."

Nash shot him a look. "You're staying in the truck when we get there. Anything happens to you, Rowan will kick my ass."

"Anything happens to her, I'll kick my own. Drive, son."

CHAPTER 12

*R*owan's muscles were cramping, but the pain from the taser had faded. Her wrists had been bound with a zip tie. The plastic dug into her skin, rubbing it raw. But she was grateful he'd gone with this instead of cuffs. Under the right circumstances, she could get out of this. As Voss currently had a gun trained on her where she was folded like a rag doll into the floorboard, these were not the right circumstances.

"Why couldn't you just leave well enough

alone?" he demanded. "I didn't want to hurt you."

"Really? Because it sounded a whole lot like you wanted Morales to shoot me."

"It would've been simpler that way. But Morales has a type, and he wanted to play with you. Trust me. Death would've been the better option."

"Cheery thought. But I know what I heard, Voss."

"Yeah. You never wavered on that. It's a shame. A damned shame. You're a good cop. An asset to the department. You'd have made a good detective someday. If you'd just fucking let it go."

Rowan's blood chilled at the past tense. "You should know that's exactly why I couldn't let it go."

Voss snorted with disgust. "You know, you and Reyes were well matched. He got in the way, too. It's just too damned bad you're going to have to meet the same fate."

"What are you saying?"

"Come on now, Beale. You're smarter than that. Reyes stuck his nose in where it didn't belong. So, Morales and his people took care of him."

The call had been a setup from the beginning. David's death had been deliberate, not just a bust gone sideways. Rowan's gut began to cramp. She'd known. Somewhere, deep down, she'd suspected this. And it had been part of why she couldn't let things go. Why she'd endured ostracism and ridicule and risked the job that she loved rather than let this piece of shit walk away unscathed. She was doing this for David.

"Why would you do it?" Tears thickened her voice, and she didn't bother fighting them back. Let him think she was overwrought. A weak, defenseless woman. She twisted her head to look at him, so he could see the tears. The gun was still on her, but it wavered a bit on the bumpy road. "Why would you betray the badge?"

"I never wanted to do that. I became a cop to

be one of the good guys. But guess what? Being one of the good guys doesn't pay for shit. It doesn't come with the kind of benefits that will pay for all the cancer treatments for my wife. I was desperate. She needed more than we could afford, or she would've been in the ground two years ago. She was already stage four when they found it."

"So, you did what? Made a deal with Morales to be their guy on the inside? What exactly are you doing for him?" He was planning to kill her anyway. Why not ask for the details?

"Tipping him off about busts, roadblocks. Quietly making evidence disappear so his key people would walk. In exchange, I got the kind of money we needed to get her into better treatment. The kind of money we needed so she'd survive."

As he spoke, Rowan shifted, curling tighter into herself until she could get her feet under her. They screamed at the angle, but that was good. That meant she had some feeling in them instead of total numbness. "So, you're doing this all for love."

"Yeah."

"How do you think your wife would feel about you crossing that line? She married the good guy with the badge. The one who upholds the law. How do you think she'd look at you if she knew what you'd done?"

"She'll never know. And at least she's still around to look at me at all."

She'd never know because Rowan was the only one who could tell her, and Voss was going to kill her. For all his protestations that he hadn't wanted to hurt her, he'd clearly gotten over whatever reservations he had.

"How does Dr. Powers fit in with this? Why is she helping you?"

"Tisha and I have an arrangement. She helped provide me with the best means of getting to you."

"And in exchange?"

"She gets to comfort me and play out that

Florence Nightingale fantasy on the emotionally wounded patient."

"You're sleeping with her."

"A means to an end. And a man needs comfort."

Had he always been this deluded? Or had he actually begun a legitimately good man and been twisted into this by desperation and circumstance? It hardly mattered. She wasn't dealing with a good man now. She was dealing with one she'd pushed to the edge, and if she didn't do something, she was dead.

"Tell me something...the gunshots last night. There were no casings, no slugs. Were you just firing into the air?"

"Fun little trick, that. It was a recording, played with a directional amplifier. Loud as hell to you, but not to anybody outside the range."

A recording. No wonder there'd been no evidence. "It almost worked. Would have worked if my uncle hadn't heard."

"I didn't realize until after that anybody else

was home. Pity. Would've saved us both a lot of trouble."

Straining her neck, she looked up at him. His gaze kept bouncing between the road and her. Past his head, she could see a smattering of naked branches mixed in with towering pine trees. "Where are you taking me?"

"There are thousands of acres of wilderness in this county. Plenty of places to hide your body where it won't be discovered until long after the trace evidence is gone. But don't worry. I'm not interested in making you suffer. I've got enough respect for you as a fellow cop to make it quick."

Rowan launched herself, slamming into Voss. The gun went off and the truck lurched wildly. He fought her, fought for control, but her body was wedged between him and the wheel. She felt rather than saw the truck leave the road and tried to throw herself back toward the other side of the seat. Then the truck crashed into a tree and everything went a blinding white before fading to blackness.

~

NASH DROVE like a bat out of hell, determined to make up the distance. He didn't let himself think of what could be happening to Rowan. Didn't let himself think of what Voss—or whoever had her—might already have done. He just focused on closing that distance and getting to her.

In the passenger seat, Robert continued to coordinate with other officers on the radio.

Did Voss have a radio himself tuned to the police band? Did he know they were coming?

The caller had reported him driving fast. So, he was in escape mode. He couldn't have had time to kill her and dump the body yet. Logic dictated Rowan was still alive. She had to be. He just had to catch up.

Careening around a curve in the county road, he caught a flash of black and hit the brakes. A truck with a camper top had plowed straight into a tree. The front end was smashed, the hood buckled. Windows were shattered.

The driver's side door hung partly open. There was no telling how fast they'd been going when they hit.

Rowan, what did you do?

Robert was already calling it in as Nash pulled up behind it.

"Stay here." He slipped out, gun drawn, edging closer to the mangled vehicle.

The winter woods were quiet, but for a breeze singing through the trees and the sound of his footsteps crunching on pine needles. Dread weighed on him like lead as he circled around to the open driver's door. There was no one inside. No broken bodies that hadn't survived the crash. The windshield was shattered but still mostly intact. No evidence a body had been thrown out the front. The airbag had deployed. It lay wilted over the steering wheel. The white fabric was streaked with blood, as was the bench seat. Was it his blood or hers? Or both?

"Somebody's bleeding pretty good," Robert observed.

"I told you to stay in the truck."

Ignoring him, Robert pointed to the ground. "Blood trail heads off that way."

"You can't come with me."

"I'm not armed. You think I'm gonna head on into the woods in my damned bedroom slippers in my condition? I'm not stupid, Brewer. Backup's on the way. Be careful. We don't know whose blood that is."

With a short nod, Nash moved into the trees. A dozen feet in he found a snapped zip tie. The sight of it spurred him faster. She was alive, and she'd broken her bonds.

I'm coming. Just hang on. I'm coming.

He had to force himself to move slowly, searching out the blood spatter on fallen leaves and listening hard for other signs of movement. Had she managed to get far enough ahead to hide? The trees here were certainly thick enough, full of undergrowth that would make the area virtually impenetrable at any other time of year. He carefully picked over thick vines and roots, backtracking when he lost the trail. Thank God it was still daylight.

He was nearly a quarter mile in when he heard the gunshot, close enough it made his ears ring. It echoed through the silence with a finality that lodged Nash's heart in his throat.

No. No no no no.

He began to run, fighting his way through the brush. He couldn't be too late. Catching movement ahead, he poured on speed and broke into a small clearing.

"Rowan!"

They were both on their feet, Rowan fighting for control of the gun in her assailant's hand. Blood stained his shoulder, but the wound didn't seem to be hampering him. He bent, trying to use his greater size to overpower her.

Nash leveled his gun. "Freeze!" They didn't, and he couldn't get a clean shot, not with Rowan right there.

Even as he watched, she dug a finger into the wound. The man howled. Impervious to the blows landing on her head and shoulders, Rowan landed a hard, sharp strike to the other man's arm. The gun fell from his fingers. With a roar, he dove forward, tackling her around the waist. Rowan landed hard on her back, her breath coming out in a woosh, and Nash could've sworn she *smiled*, even as her attacker drove a fist into her ribs.

Quick as a snake, she grabbed fistfuls of the other man's shirt, lifted her hips, and rolled. It was the same move she'd used on Nash the day they'd sparred. Suddenly she was on top. He bucked, trying to roll, punching at whatever he could hit, but she kept the upper hand. Her hands wrapped around his throat, and she began to squeeze. And at last, with her arms locked out, Nash had a clean shot.

"Give it up, or I'm gonna put a bullet in your brain."

"Need him alive to prosecute." Rowan grunted as she took more blows to the ribs.

"Then you might want to stop squeezing so hard."

The man's face was turning an alarming shade of red and the punches he aimed at Rowan's sides were more like flailing.

"I suggest you cooperate, Voss. Because I promise you my friend here would be a lot happier shooting you for having kidnapped me."

With a baleful look at Nash, Voss stopped fighting.

"Got cuffs?" she asked.

Nash pulled them off his duty belt. He walked close enough to toss them to her, but not close enough that Voss could reach out and grab at him. "You okay?"

Rowan shifted her grip and reached up with one hand to snatch them. "I'm sure I've got an assortment of bruises and scrapes and probably some burns from the airbag, but I'll be fine." She snapped the cuffs on one wrist and began reciting his rights as she efficiently rolled him to his belly, twisting his arm behind his back with more force than strictly necessary. "Trent Voss, you're under arrest." Voss cried out between gasps. Rowan finished cuffing him, then fell back on her ass, breathing hard. She shifted triumphant blue eyes up to Nash. "What took you so long?"

God, he was crazy about this woman.

"I stopped to pick up Chief Grumpy."

Her eyes widened. "Robert's with you?"

"Back at the truck, waiting on backup." The faint wail of a siren sounded in the distance. "Guess they're nearly here." Holstering his weapon, Nash strode over to where she sat and offered his hand.

As soon as she placed hers in his, he tugged her to her feet and straight into his arms. She burrowed in, holding every bit as tight as he did. If his embrace bothered any of her injuries, she didn't make a sound.

"I thought I was too late." He worked on swallowing down the heart that was still hammering in his throat. "But I guess you had it under control."

"If you're going to date me, Nash, you're really going to have to get used to the fact that I can handle myself."

When he was sure he could put on the cocky smile she wanted, he pulled back a little. "I'm gonna date you?"

"I figured you would since I'm planning to try to move here."

"Thank God."

She lifted her head from his chest. "In all seriousness, I should've listened to you. If I hadn't been on my own, he never would've gotten to me."

"If you're gonna date me, you're gonna have to learn that you're not alone anymore. I've got your six. Always."

Her smile bloomed, and it was the best damned thing Nash had seen in weeks. "If you're gonna kiss me, you should probably do it fast before my prospective future colleagues arrive. For propriety and stuff."

"Screw propriety," he said, and captured her mouth with his.

EPILOGUE

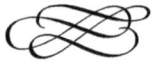

owan's hands shook a bit as she buttoned up the new uniform shirt. The starched fabric scraped against her skin, reminding her that this was a beginning. One where she'd be starting over in nearly every sense of the word. The newest officer on a tiny force. The only woman. It was imperative she make a good impression.

So, she'd shined her shoes to a mirror gleam and put creases in her navy pants sharp enough to cut. Her hair was pulled back in a severe bun that added a few years to the face she knew still looked young, despite the college degree and six years of experience on the job. Her new badge rode proud above her left breast. As a last step, she slipped on her duty belt. The familiar weight of it settled around her hips, a welcome anchor as she stepped into uncharted waters.

Rowan smoothed down her tie. The woman in the mirror was the one she'd been fighting to get back to. After the past few months, she almost felt like a stranger. Maybe it would feel different after the swearing in today.

"Ready to go?"

"Yes, sir." Rowan nodded, more at her reflection than her great uncle, and turned.

He stood in the doorway, shoulders straight in a sport coat, his brown hair still damp from a shower. Two months out from his bypass surgery, he looked almost himself again. It would still be a while before he was as active as he wanted to be, but she no longer had to play warden.

"Nervous?" Of course, he'd see that. No one knew her like Uncle Robert.

"A little. I know it's not the same, but this was your department, your people. You left big shoes to fill."

"You're more than up to the task. And if he didn't think you were qualified, Ethan wouldn't have hired you."

True enough. But it wasn't her new boss who worried her.

The drive to City Hall only took ten minutes, but it felt like an hour. Her hands were actually a little bit clammy as they climbed out and made their way to the conference room on the second floor. She surreptitiously wiped her palms on her pants before they entered the room, and she was introduced to Mayor Sandra Peyton and the members of the City Council. Chief Greer was also in attendance, but he was the only one from her new department.

Rowan herself seemed to be the only one with a steel rod in her spine. As her great uncle chatted with these people he'd known for years, she stood at military attention, wishing they'd just get this show on the road.

"At ease, Officer Beale."

The murmured voice had her shoulders tensing momentarily in surprise before melting in relief. Nash had come.

"Sorry I'm late. My client ran late, so I was almost an hour past my planned return. It's possible I used my dash lights to get here on time without getting a ticket."

Rowan kept her voice low, her eyes on the assembly. "I'm not sworn in yet, so I guess we can overlook that gross misuse of power."

"The uniform looks good on you."

She just hoped the new position fit as well.

Mayor Peyton smiled. "Well, shall we get started with the formalities?"

"Yes, ma'am." Rowan stepped to the head of the table as everyone else took a seat. Everyone but Robert, who had the honor of holding the Bible. His look of pride as she laid her left hand on the worn leather tome warmed her down to her toes.

The mayor's smooth voice filled the sudden quiet. "Please raise your right hand."

She did as instructed and repeated the oath she was given. "I, Rowan Beale, do solemnly swear and confirm that I will support, protect, and defend the Constitution and government of the United States, the State of Mississippi, and the city of Wishful..." With every word spoken, her voice gained confidence, ringing out in the small room. "I will bear truth, loyalty, and allegiance to the same, and I will honorably and faithfully perform the duties of a police officer, so help me God."

She signed the necessary paperwork. Then it was over, and the mayor was clasping her hand. "Congratulations, Officer Beale, and welcome to Wishful!"

Short and sweet. Thank God.

She ran the gauntlet of handshakes, posed for the obligatory pictures for the paper with the mayor and Chief Greer. The photographer even took one of her with Robert, saying they wanted to do a story in the *Observer* about her connection to their much-beloved former Chief of Police. She hesitated at that. There might be some who believed he was why she'd gotten the job. But after all the years she'd come here, all the stories she'd heard, she realized that for most, that connection would lead to greater acceptance, so she agreed to a brief interview later in the week.

Ethan crossed his arms. "Well, Beale, you ready for your first day on the job?"

"Absolutely, sir."

Amusement flickered across his features as he looked to Nash. "How long do you think it'll take to break her of all this formality?"

"At least a couple of weeks." He grinned.

"You coming in for the briefing?" Ethan asked.

Nash nodded, all businesslike, but Rowan didn't miss the smile flirting at the corners of his mouth.

"You're up to something," she accused as they made their way downstairs.

"Don't know what you're talking about. See you at the briefing in a bit." Before she could say anything else, he'd peeled off from the group and headed to his truck.

"I'll drive you," Robert said. "Figure I'll stop in and say hello to Inez and whoever's around."

"So glad you're with me on the first day of school, Dad."

Robert's lips twitched. "Might as well be a little like that. Proud of you, Roo. And I'm self-ishly glad you decided to apply for the job here. I got used to having you around."

"I like having you around, too."

From all the cars in the small lot of the police station, it looked like everyone had come for this morning's briefing. The nerves came back with a vengeance. Rowan braced herself to walk in, wondering what these men would think about her—the woman who'd held the law higher than the brotherhood.

Voss had been arrested, along with two other officers found to be involved in the scheme. Dr. Powers had lost her license and been charged as an accessory. The trial was coming up, and until it was over, the stain of the whole sordid mess would follow her around like a storm cloud. She just hoped her new coworkers would be able to overlook it.

"Does it feel weird coming back here and not being Chief?"

"A bit. But turns out I get to still show up for the important stuff." On that cryptic remark, he opened the door for her.

Rowan stepped through and stopped cold at the chorus of cheerful brays from a collection of paper noisemakers. A banner stretched across the room: Welcome Officer Beale! Beneath it, every member of the department, including Nash and Reuben, stood in a grinning cluster.

Offering a cautious smile, she stepped forward. "What's all this?"

"A welcome to the department party," Ethan said.

"There's even cake from Sweet Magnolias!" Inez proudly gestured to a nearby table sporting a cake shaped like a Wishful PD badge. Closer inspection showed it was her badge number iced on the top. The whole thing felt a little unreal.

"Y'all did all this for me?"

Nash rubbed her shoulder. "One of the selling points we didn't mention when suggesting you apply for the job is that a small-town department is more than just a place to work. It's a family. And you're now part of ours."

A knot clogged up Rowan's throat, and she wished she wasn't at work so she could turn into Nash and hug him. Instead, she swallowed back the lump and turned to face her new coworkers—her new family. "Thank you, all of you, for this welcome. It means a lot to me."

Inez brandished a cake knife. "Y'all better eat fast before the next calls come in."

Rowan had first pick—corner piece, of course. They got approximately five minutes to eat and socialize before the phone rang. Corbett and Clint, the two officers besides Rowan officially on duty, shoveled their cake in faster.

"Yes ma'am, Mrs. Ramsey, I'll send someone

right out," Inez promised. She hung up. "Chester Harkin's horses got out again, and Miss Maudie Bell is on the warpath."

Rowan started to set her cake aside, but Clint just lifted a staying hand. "Finish your cake. We'll take one for the team. Corbett?"

The rookie set his cake aside. "I'm ready."

Rowan watched in amusement as the pair of them played Rock, Paper, Scissors to decide who had to take the call. Corbett won with paper over rock.

Clint grimaced. "Maybe she won't try to pinch my ass this time."

Rowan went brows up. "Do you normally have trouble with sexual harassment from citizens?"

Nash laughed. "Oh, this isn't sexual harassment. This is the Casserole Patrol."

"The...Casserole Patrol?" she repeated.

"You'll learn, Beale. You'll learn." Clint saluted. "Welcome to the department."

When he'd gone, Nash nudged her back toward the break room. "You need a refill on that iced tea."

She didn't, but she could tell he had more than beverages on his mind and didn't mind stealing a moment of privacy, despite the uniform. He shut the door behind them.

"Subtle," she said.

"The propriety's just for you. Everybody knows we're dating."

"So considerate." Rowan lifted her arms to his shoulders as he stepped in. "This was all your idea, wasn't it?"

"I might've put a bug in some ears, but they did most of it on their own. I knew you were nervous, and I wanted your first day to go well."

"I appreciate it."

Nash grinned. "I can think of a few ways you could express that appreciation."

Rowan was definitely amenable to those, but as he bent to kiss her, she couldn't resist teasing him. "So, if this is a family, does that make you my brother?"

That familiar heated look in his brown eyes

had her toes curling inside her standard issue shoes. "It most emphatically does not."

And he tipped his mouth to hers and proved it.

~

CHOOSE YOUR NEXT ROMANCE

ARE you in the mood for more of the Wishful PD? On deck next is our brand new police chief, Ethan Greer. In *Can't Take My Eyes Off You* he meets his match in the stubborn Miranda Campbell. If you're a fan of my Wishful Romance series, you've probably been wondering when Miranda was gonna meet her match. This right here is the best friend story you've been waiting for. It's full of plenty of Campbell crazy, serenades, and a hefty dose of hair-raising danger. Don't miss it!

Grab your copy of *Can't Take My Eyes Off You* today.

OTHER BOOKS BY KAIT NOLAN

A complete and up-to-date list of all my books can be found at https://kaitnolan.com.

THE MISFIT INN SERIES
SMALL TOWN FAMILY ROMANCE

- *When You Got A Good Thing* (Kennedy and Xander)
- *Til There Was You* (Misty and Denver)

- *Those Sweet Words* (Pru and Flynn)
- *Stay A Little Longer* (Athena and Logan)
- *Bring It On Home* (Maggie and Porter)

RESCUE MY HEART SERIES
SMALL TOWN MILITARY ROMANCE

- *Baby It's Cold Outside* (Ivy and Harrison)
- *What I Like About You* (Laurel and Sebastian)
- *Bad Case of Loving You* (Paisley and Ty prequel)
- *Made For Loving You* (Paisley and Ty)

MEN OF THE MISFIT INN
SMALL TOWN SOUTHERN ROMANCE

- *Let It Be Me* (Emerson and Caleb)
- *Our Kind of Love* (Abbey and Kyle)

WISHFUL SERIES

SMALL TOWN SOUTHERN ROMANCE

- *Once Upon A Coffee* (Avery and Dillon)
- *To Get Me To You* (Cam and Norah)
- *Know Me Well* (Liam and Riley)
- *Be Careful, It's My Heart* (Brody and Tyler)
- *Just For This Moment* (Myles and Piper)
- *Wish I Might* (Reed and Cecily)
- *Turn My World Around* (Tucker and Corinne)
- *Dance Me A Dream* (Jace and Tara)
- *See You Again* (Trey and Sandy)
- *The Christmas Fountain* (Chad and Mary Alice)
- *You Were Meant For Me* (Mitch and Tess)
- *A Lot Like Christmas* (Ryan and Hannah)
- *Dancing Away With My Heart* (Zach and Lexi)

WISHING FOR A HERO SERIES (A WISHFUL SPINOFF SERIES)
SMALL TOWN ROMANTIC SUSPENSE

- *Make You Feel My Love* (Judd and Autumn)
- *Watch Over Me* (Nash and Rowan)
- *Can't Take My Eyes Off You* (Ethan and Miranda)
- *Burn For You* (Sean and Delaney)

MEET CUTE ROMANCE
SMALL TOWN SHORT ROMANCE

- *Once Upon A Snow Day*
- *Once Upon A New Year's Eve*
- *Once Upon An Heirloom*
- *Once Upon A Coffee*
- *Once Upon A Campfire*
- *Once Upon A Rescue*

SUMMER CAMP
CONTEMPORARY ROMANCE

- *Once Upon A Campfire*
- *Second Chance Summer*

ABOUT KAIT

Kait is a Mississippi native, who often swears like a sailor, calls everyone sugar, honey, or darlin', and can wield a bless your heart like a saber or a Snuggie, depending on requirements.

You can find more information on this

RITA ® Award-winning author and her books on her website http://kaitnolan.com. While you're there, sign up for her newsletter so you don't miss out on news about new releases!

www.ingramcontent.com/pod-product-compliance
Lightning Source LLC
Chambersburg PA
CBHW070531100726

47907CB00004B/1066